Monkey
Shines

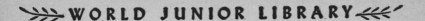

⇛⇛⇛ **WORLD JUNIOR LIBRARY** ⇚⇚⇚

Monkey Shines

by EARL SCHENCK MIERS

Illustrated by PAUL GALDONE

CLEVELAND · NEW YORK

THE WORLD PUBLISHING COMPANY

Library of Congress Catalog Card Number: 52–8423

HC 755

For

MR. TROUBLE

and

JOANNA

who are very much alive!

Contents

Illustrations

Monkey
Shines

1 The Price
of a Bulldozer

POKE JOHNSON waved his arm toward the blackberry bushes. "Right there," he said, "is where we'll put third base."

"And right here," answered Turkey Saunders, "is where I go home!"

Whether Turkey felt indignant or simply disgusted was difficult to tell. As far as Turkey knew, those bushes had been growing in the old meadow since the year Noah set the Ark on dry land, and if their roots didn't reach to China, a sprout or two must have penetrated almost to Tibet! Turkey could see himself yanking at those brambles until his hands bled.

"Sometimes," he told Poke, "your head gets as mushy as a soft-boiled egg!"

Poke laughed. With the June sun beating down as though it held a grudge against the earth, Turkey could be right. But Poke was squat and chunky where Turkey was thin and scrawny, so that the sun had more of Poke than of Turkey

3

to bedevil—a fact, the stout boy decided, that gave him an edge in the dispute.

"The trouble with you," Poke said, "is that where it takes a blowgun to puncture my hide, your tender skin buckles under the *ping* of a pea-shooter. Now use a bit of imagination, Turk. This old meadow can be turned into a first-class ball field. With a little work—"

"A *little* work!" When Turkey swallowed, sometimes his Adam's apple bobbed up and down so that it resembled a mole burrowing in furious pursuit of an earthworm. With fascination, Poke followed the rhythmical convolutions of Turkey's throat as the scrawny boy sputtered on:

"Look at this place! Those bushes aren't the worst of it. See that low spot over where first would be? After a heavy rain a guy could drown himself sliding back into base! An' look at those clumps you'd have to clear away in the outfield—honest, a self-respecting cow would stick up her nose at this meadow!"

Under the worst circumstances, Poke didn't fancy himself any dumber than a bovine. He replied with a hint of stubbornness, "We'll put it up to Sleepy!"

The two boys, breaking off their argument, turned toward a nearby shady glen where a companion stretched lazily on the ground.

Sleepy Jones presented a remarkable demonstration of mechanized repose. By crossing the legs of a pair of well-patched dungarees, Sleepy's foot swung forward and back with a kind of monotonous, effortless motion, and at the same time a long blade of grass, held loosely between his teeth, could be manipulated by the slightest pressure of the tongue to fan the tip of Sleepy's freckled nose. For stray flies, curious gnats, bothersome bees, nosy ants, and simple-minded butterflies, the swinging foot and the blade of grass supplied eloquent warning that here rested a person who would not surrender without a fight his inalienable right to life, liberty, and the pursuit of long periods of uninterrupted leisure.

At the age of eleven, Sleepy Jones had become a Northfield tradition. Other towns could claim among their inhabitants, living or dead, a senator or an author or a horse thief, but Northfield alone had raised and harbored Sleepy. Understandably there were some to whom Sleepy seemed a trial, including the progression of teachers who had taught Sleepy in the school on Maple Avenue. They would behold Sleepy sitting at his desk, his face masked with a kind of goofy benignity, and no teacher ever had been sure whether Sleepy's eyes really were open or shut, or whether he was partly awake or entirely asleep. No teacher, certain that she had divined the truth, ever had surprised Sleepy with a question hurled at him like one of Jove's thunderbolts. Every time Sleepy revealed that he already had seen what had been written on the blackboard and now only waited patiently for the teacher to catch up to him. In a way, Sleepy could be exasperating. But not in Poke's opinion. He'd like to have half of Sleepy's brains even if half of Sleepy's freckles had to go with them. Poke addressed the reclining boy with a note of respect.

"Old Beauty Rest, you heard Turkey an' me. What do you think?"

"I heard," admitted Sleepy, "and felt sorrow for your parents. What a mentally retarded pair you two are! In short, you're nuts!"

"Are you going to spend all summer trying to make a ball field out of this meadow?" Turkey demanded, while his mole of an Adam's apple burrowed madly after the earthworm.

"Of course not!"

"See?" Turkey ribbed Poke exultantly. "Out of the mouths of babes—and groundhogs—comes wisdom!"

Poke looked crestfallen. "Unless we have a home ball field," he said, "there'll be no Northfield team in the county's new Little League. Darn! Maybe Northfield is just a little jerkwater crossroads to some people, but we'd have shown 'em!"

"Maybe they would have shown us," said Turkey, who never knew when to let up.

Poke's nose twitched with annoyance. The stout boy had been talking up the idea of a Northfield team in the new league since before school closed. The Little League movement had swept the country because it cut down baseball to the size of fellows their age. With bases sixty feet apart, the pitcher's mound forty-four feet from home plate, and a ball slightly larger than a big league ball, a Little League game claimed everything: speed, action, skill!

Poke had thought of the old meadow and his dream of a Northfield team in the league had grown brighter, but now everything appeared ruined. Hang Turkey—if the truth were known, he probably had decided that the whole proposition was too big for them! Perhaps compared to places like Culver City, Newton, and Franklinville, Northfield was only a flea on the back of a hound dog, but nine guys playing together, wanting to win because the odds were against 'em . . .

At the shattered vision Poke sighed, long and sadly, like a balloon with a slow leak.

Sleepy's foot came to a halt and the blade of grass ceased

twitching. "It wouldn't be so tough," he said. "A couple of hours an' most of the work would be done."

Poke broke in excitedly: "Sleepy, do you think—"

"That this meadow can be made into a ball field good enough for the Little League? Sure! All we need is your dad's consent, since he owns the meadow—and a bulldozer!"

"Holy cow!" snorted Turkey. "Only a bulldozer? No atomic energy? No Georgia chain gang to do the work?"

Sleepy's eyes bestowed on Turkey the kind of glance usually reserved for a nettlesome mosquito. "Bulldozers exist," he said. "Right here in Northfield. In fact, there are a couple of 'em being used on that highway they're building through here to link up with the Culver City Parkway!"

"Do you know what it costs to hire a bulldozer?"

"Do you?"

"More dough than we've got!"

"Money! That's all anybody ever thinks about when there's something to be done!" Turkey's jibes had begun to ruffle Sleepy to the point where he sat up and waggled the blade of grass angrily.

"You got a good substitute for money?" Turkey asked in cool disdain.

"Who needs money?" Sleepy shot back recklessly. "If you go at a thing the right way, you don't need to line your pockets with gold."

"It'll help."

"When Washington crossed the Delaware he needed rowboats and not sawbucks," Sleepy orated with a burst of home-brewed logic. "An' if we want a bulldozer what we need most is persuasion!"

"Who," Turkey demanded, "is goin' to do all this persuadin'?"

The moment Sleepy snapped, "*I am!*" he realized that he should have shut his big yap. But Turkey made him mad —Turkey always talked a thing down instead of up—and in this respect he was even worse than Poke, who always thought you could fly a kite at least as high as the moon. Turkey's cynical smile said, "Empty barrels make the most noise," and Sleepy wondered if for once maybe Turkey wasn't right. Next time, Sleepy decided, he'd remain playing possum and keep out of trouble!

"If anybody can do it, Sleepy can!" Poke proclaimed gleefully.

The boy on the ground winced. An inner stirring told him that it must be close to lunchtime, and he wasn't sorry. Five minutes more of Turkey's ribbing, and he'd be offering to float across the Atlantic Ocean on an automobile inner tube!

When at last Sleepy stood erect, stifling a final yawn, Turkey said, "Too bad you aren't a Texan, Sleepy. They go in for tall yarns down thataway!"

"Uh-huh," Sleepy answered. "I'm going home to eat and I can't say I'm sorry that you're heading thisaway while I'll be travelin' thataway!"

With dignity Sleepy skirted a puddle and loped off across the old meadow.

2 All Sizes
of Trouble

ALONG MAPLE AVENUE the odor of fresh-cut grass blended sweetly with the scent of the flowering magnolias, but Sleepy's spirits remained depressed. The problem of how to secure *by persuasion alone* the services of a bulldozer weighed heavily on his young shoulders.

Better times have been known for a three-year-old brother, charging down the sidewalk on a tricycle, to decide that Sleepy's legs were shaped like a tunnel. On his birth certificate the three-year-old was called William Dodsworth Jones, but Sleepy had nicknamed the younger boy Mr. Trouble, for reasons that immediately became clear.

Sleepy felt himself lifted, carried backward, and dumped ingloriously on the end of his spine. The tricycle careened across his chest before hitting a tree. And Mr. Trouble, flung atop a privet hedge, hung there crying, "Bumps! More bumps!"

"I'll give you more bumps," Sleepy muttered. "Right on your fanny!"

Then Sleepy laughed. Mr. Trouble possessed spunk and

9

get-up-and-go, two qualities that Sleepy admired very much as long as they could be managed in a restful manner. Mr. Trouble had more spunk than Turkey Saunders, Sleepy told himself, and since Sleepy was no closer to a scheme for securing the services of that bulldozer he concentrated on all his reasons for disliking Turkey.

Perhaps "dislike" was too strong a word, but Turkey did irritate him. Not the way Mr. Trouble bothered him by always being underfoot. Turkey got under his skin. And yet, why? Pressed to say explicitly why Turkey annoyed him, Sleepy couldn't, but a feeling of irksomeness with Turkey persisted.

Sleepy mounted the porch steps of the Jones residence under some difficulty, insofar as Mr. Trouble succeeded in constantly entangling himself in the older boy's legs. The clatter of pans and dishes in the kitchen, where Mrs. Jones prepared luncheon, led Sleepy to steel himself against an almost certain outburst: "Sleepy, you get upstairs and wash —mind, get behind your ears—and, Sleepy Jones, no dirt under your fingernails or I'll do the scrubbing!"

At times, Sleepy thought, there were advantages to being a deaf mute. When he entered the cool living room, there sat his father, home early from the store and reading a book. Sleepy dropped down on the sofa beside him.

"I saw Mr. Trouble run you down," Mr. Jones said. "I like the way you took it."

"Kids his age aren't responsible."

Mr. Jones smiled. "Sleepy," he said, "that's almost the most grown-up remark you've ever made."

Sleepy felt pleased. Sometimes Sleepy's mother needled him about not helping his father around the store, but what boy wanted to spend his summer vacation behind the counter of a musty old hardware establishment? Brooms and rakes and electric light fixtures and boxes of screws and bolts—who could grow excited over that junk? Sleepy's mother accused him of being lazy and Sleepy cheerfully admitted that he was, in some ways.

Still, a sense of guiltiness often gnawed at Sleepy. There were streaks of gray in Mr. Jones's hair and at some moments the tired lines under his eyes seemed deep. But Mr. Jones never asked Sleepy to come around to the store, and the boy reasoned that if his father really wanted his help he'd say so. What Sleepy liked most about his father was the fact that his dad never intervened in Sleepy's private affairs unless the boy asked him. Today Sleepy very definitely wanted advice.

"Who's building the new highway?" he asked.

"The Kyler Construction Company."

"Know anything about them?"

"Buzz Kyler is their president."

That name, Sleepy reflected, had a familiar ring—and then, as though Mr. Trouble had jabbed him with a fork, Sleepy sat up. "You mean the Buzz Kyler who used to play with the New York Yankees?"

Mr. Jones nodded.

"The one who hit the grand-slam home run to break up the World Series game with the Brooklyn Dodgers a couple of seasons ago?"

"The same old Buzz. As a matter of fact, he likes Northfield so much he's going to move here permanently."

"No kiddin'?"

"I guess you could say that we had gained a celebrity,"

Mr. Jones continued. "Buzz went fast once he began to fade, but for a long time he was in the front rank of the stars."

He sure was, Sleepy agreed. The boy could have laughed aloud, considering how simply he had turned the tables on Turkey Saunders! Getting that bulldozer from Buzz Kyler to

"What is it, kid?"

help build a baseball field should be a cinch! So much of the goodness of life engulfed Sleepy that he told his father: "I guess I better go up and wash before lunch!" And splashing water over his face—the preliminary step to wiping off most of the dirt on the towel—Sleepy reflected how in a

pinch his dad always came through with the right answer. There was nothing showy about his dad, but then, the boy guessed, the thing that gave the Rock of Gibraltar its reputation was its strength and not its appearance. A good guy, thought Sleepy, hanging the towel where he usually did—on the floor.

An hour later Sleepy walked with a light tread along the road where the trucks, steam shovels, and bulldozers of the Kyler Construction Company rumbled and roared. Clouds of yellow dust rolled over the countryside, but the vision that had seized Sleepy remained undimmed.

The boy remembered the pictures that he had seen so often in the newspapers—big Buzz Kyler, built like a Paul Bunyan, who had handled a Louisville slugger better than most cops could swing a nightstick. One season Buzz had hit forty-nine home runs, the next fifty-two. When Buzz went after a ball in the field, the sports writers had said, he was as fleet as a rabbit; and his big mitt, reaching up, had scooped flies off the wall as though the glove had been a butterfly net. Ty Cobb, Babe Ruth, Joe DiMaggio—that was the class to which Buzz Kyler belonged!

Sleepy sighed. Who knew? Maybe Buzz Kyler would coach the Northfield team! Think what that would mean! Why, with Buzz Kyler behind them, giving them pointers, they'd be the scourge of the Little League. They'd wipe up Culver City, Newton, and Franklinville! Sleepy chuckled. Did he say "wipe"? Brother, they'd *mop* 'em up—with a wringer and a pail!

It wasn't difficult for Sleepy to spot Buzz. Even out of a Yankee uniform, no one could mistake that husky, powerful figure. Look at that guy—built solid, right from the ground!

Then Sleepy stood not half a dozen feet away from where Buzz directed the highway construction job, and the boy seemed to grow tongue-tied. Once, twice, he opened his mouth to say something that would attract the great outfielder's notice, but no words emerged. Feeling foolish, Sleepy twisted his foot in the dirt and tried once more.

"Er, Buzz—I mean, Mr. Kyler."

The big man turned around. "What is it, kid?"

Sleepy wished that Buzz's tone sounded more cordial. "Could I—could I ask you a question?" Sleepy managed at last.

"Well, spit it out," the great Buzz Kyler said. "I haven't got all day."

Right then Sleepy knew his defeat. But some stubborn quality in Sleepy forced him to voice his request. He was perspiring when he finished.

Buzz Kyler hitched his thumbs under his belt and scowled down at the boy.

"Look, kid," he said, "I'm in the construction business to make money an' not to play Santa Claus to a bunch of ragamuffins. We're working here, see? If you'll take my advice, you'll beat it before somebody gets careless with a bulldozer an' buries you under a pile of dirt!"

Something in the curt, unnecessarily harsh way Buzz spoke slashed Sleepy's pride like a whip. Angry tears stung the fringes of his eyes, but he forced them back. He turned on his heels, and not until then did he recognize another boy of about his own age watching from the cab of one of the steam shovels.

"Hello," the other boy said.

"Hi," Sleepy responded sullenly.

"Anything I can do?"

"No," Sleepy began, but then his disappointment and disillusionment, the unjustified sense of shame he had been made to feel, settled in a hard knot in the pit of his stomach. Impulsively he jerked his head toward Buzz Kyler.

"Maybe," he asked the boy in the cab, "you can tell me why such a champ like that turns out to be so big a chump!"

Without waiting for an answer, Sleepy's long, angry strides carried him back along the road.

3 The Secret
of the Meadow

SOMETHING *had* to be wrong. Rolling in bed and listening to the rising, flute-like song of a hermit thrush, Sleepy tried to recall the last time he had been awake at daybreak. Even Mr. Trouble slumbered soundly, and Sleepy, disturbed by the tremendous silence of the old house, called himself an idiot for the way he had been bothered by Buzz Kyler.

"That guy," Sleepy told himself disgustedly, "will go down in history as Northfield's great A-Number-1 fizzle!"

Sleepy's umbrage (the fanciest word he knew for being sore as a skinned cat) mounted. Northfield was a nice town, where everyone was friendly, and its population certainly wouldn't be enhanced by the arrival of anyone who responded to a civil request as though you were forty-seven kinds of a bum! Buzz couldn't have shaken him off more forcefully, Sleepy decided, if he—Sleepy—had been an old shoe that had begun to pinch in all the wrong places.

Underneath it wasn't the personal rebuff that troubled Sleepy. Few endeavors in life could rouse his dormant ambition like baseball. A fellow like Poke had the chunky build of a catcher, and Turkey usually wanted to pitch, but Sleepy just naturally seemed to belong at first base. Simply having the height didn't make a first baseman, either. It took something more—a first baseman's heart.

Sleepy had thought many hours about playing first base, for frequently when others believed that Sleepy catnapped his mind played hare-and-hounds with problems like this. The thrill in covering first wasn't merely in scooping a bad throw out of the dirt, or knocking down a liner and beating the runner to the sack, or holding a guy so tight to the base that he couldn't get the jump on you and steal. There was one thing else—the pride of knowing that this was your hunk of earth and you'd protect it with your life. That was what baseball should be.

And what had Buzz's behavior done but made the game seem cheap—not something that called for the best a fellow could give, but something that was cold and remote and didn't matter unless you could place a money value on it?

At least Turkey Saunders should be satisfied. Turkey never had believed that he would get that bulldozer any more than Turkey had believed that Northfield could have much of a team in the Little League. Sleepy's resentment took a new twist. He couldn't do anything about Buzz, but Turkey was an apple he could polish. Somehow they were going to have that ball field and that team! Sleepy liked this resolution except for one detail. How would he bring these achievements into being?

Sleepy stirred restlessly. What could a fellow do when he woke up this early? He considered the possibility of dressing and creeping down to the kitchen to cook his own breakfast, but the prospect of all that effort when everyone else slept possessed scant attraction. Once more Sleepy rolled over and listened to the hermit thrush. A moment later the boy had bolted out of bed with such alacrity that the mattress bounced on the springs.

At the window Sleepy cocked his ear with intentness. But there could be no doubt that the sound coming from the meadow was the roar of a bulldozer!

Within seconds Sleepy had donned dungarees, sports shirt, and sneakers, and charged down the backstairs. The door slammed and the boy fled across the dew-covered grass.

The scene that met Sleepy's gaze when he reached the meadow caused him to stand still and blink in wonderment. The blackberry bushes had disappeared and the quagmire behind first base had been filled in! The bulldozer had made a circuit across the lower meadow and left in its wake one of the most beautiful patterns for an infield Sleepy ever had seen. The wide, sweeping arc of the base path from first to third sang out B-A-S-E-B-A-L-L as lustily as though the throats of a thousand hermit thrushes had joined in the chorus.

"This," breathed Sleepy, "is super-terrific!"

And it was. Yankee Stadium or Fenway Park or Ebbets Field never had looked more like a ball field than Poke's old meadow in the early morning sunlight. The bulldozer groaned furiously and spewed up clouds of dust as it attacked the grass clumps cluttering the outfield. Sleepy grinned. Progress—it was wonderful!

A red-faced, perspiring Irishman manipulated the wheel of the bulldozer, and beside him sat the trim-built lad who the previous afternoon had spoken to Sleepy from the cab of the steam shovel.

The Irishman was full of complaints.

"Faith, 'tis early in the day for a man in his right mind to be up! Ye young rascal, teasin' me into this nonsense was a verra risky business an' ye know it! If I'm not losin' me job over this, it will only be because I'm a monkey's uncle!"

Beside the protesting man, the boy laughed. "Faith, Kelly," he mimicked, "if I were a monkey I'm not too sure I'd be wantin' ye for me uncle!" Then, glancing down at Sleepy, he asked, "How do you like your ball field?"

Sleepy liked the field about the way Mr. Trouble enjoyed the cool, sweet drip of an ice cream cone. But all Sleepy could say was, "Gosh—it's fine!"

The boy on the bulldozer extended his hand. "I'm Johnny Kyler."

Sleepy's mental processes did one of those double somersaults that are all right when swimming but have distinct disadvantages on dry land. Johnny Kyler! Then this boy must be Buzz Kyler's son! And yesterday he had asked Johnny why his father had to be such a big chump! Sleepy's face reddened like a push-in cigarette lighter on an automobile's dashboard.

Johnny Kyler spoke softly. "You didn't understand."

Sleepy answered miserably, "Gosh, Johnny, I'm sorry. I— I—"

"Pop can be tough. I guess he took you by surprise."

"He sure did."

"How much do you remember about my dad?"

"I guess everybody remembers that grand-slam homer in the World Series," Sleepy said.

Johnny smiled. "Then maybe the rest doesn't matter!"

Sleepy looked up quizzically. What was Johnny trying to tell him? The eyes of the boy on the bulldozer glanced away, as though afraid to pursue the issue further.

"Let's forget the whole thing," he said. "You've got your

ball field—compliments of the Kyler Construction Company, you might say—and now I'd like you to keep that fact to yourself!"

In the strained silence that followed, the Irishman suggested, "We better clean up this job, Johnny, an' get out o' here!"

"Right-o," the boy answered.

Grinding, snorting, bucking, the bulldozer charged into another of the stubborn grass clumps. Sleepy watched, puzzled. Why had Buzz refused the use of the bulldozer and then permitted Johnny and his Irish companion to borrow it? What was the reason for pledging him to secrecy over the fact that the Kyler Construction Company had leveled off the old meadow? Obviously something in Buzz's past was involved with all this secrecy, but apparently Johnny had revealed all that he intended—again, why?

Sleepy scratched his head, but found no bumps of knowledge to enlighten him. The bulldozer chugged through a mound of hard-caked mud, and Sleepy, watching Johnny set the plow-end against another such mound, decided that at least he could be sure on one count:

"I like that guy!"

4 The Bogus Hero

POKE JOHNSON stuck his hand into his blouse in a Napoleonic pose and spoke with mock dignity:

"Who's always putting Northfield on the map and should be elected mayor of the old dump? Fellow countrymen, I give you the one, the only, the won't-take-no-for-an-answer wizard of this cow patch, the Honorable Sleepy Jones!"

Even Turkey Saunders could not disguise his admiration. "By jinks, I misjudged you, Sleepy. With your brand of persuasion some day you'll be President of the United States!"

Sleepy knew in his heart that he was a bogus hero. Actually he hadn't done anything but lose his temper, and that seemed a funny reason for becoming a man of the hour.

The manner in which the meadow had changed overnight from a worn-out field that even the cows disparaged into a real diamond produced an electrifying effect. Fellows like Hutch Bannister and Lover Carmichael, Asphalt Smith and Tennessee Martin suddenly decided that a summer in Northfield needn't be compared to residence in a leper colony as long as you could play baseball.

Asphalt, whose dad owned the lumber yard, promised the boards to build the team benches. And Lover—so named for his recitation in school one day of "My love is like a red, red rose" with such shrill vehemence that most of the roses for miles around withered on their bushes (or so Asphalt declared)—pledged himself to beg, borrow, or abscond with the wire for a backstop.

The festival spirit that had infected the old meadow made Poke giddy.

"Northfield," the stout boy exclaimed, "will be the toast of the county. Buttered on both sides. Golden at the edges. Nourishing to the appetite. Kind to the pocketbook. Wholesome as the morning dew—"

How much longer Poke might have held out no one ever knew. Lover Carmichael ended the poetic outburst by flipping a captured grasshopper into Poke's open mouth.

Sleepy grinned. In the commotion of Poke's wheezing pursuit of Lover, Sleepy forgot that he was a bogus hero and concentrated on how that morning the elements of a good Northfield nine were being drawn together. When shortly afterward sides were chosen for a game, redheaded Hutch Bannister covered short on Sleepy's team. Hutch, almost as badly bowlegged as a broncobuster, played his position gamely, stopping grounders when he could with his glove, but otherwise stopping the ball with his arms, legs, chest—or head.

You had to admire Hutch, Sleepy thought. He wasn't afraid to try. Nothing but Hutch's willingness to take a chance really distinguished the boy. Unlike Poke he wasn't fat, and unlike Turkey he wasn't scrawny. All Hutch could claim in life was an ability to spread himself across the ground, and hope. "But he's got spark," Sleepy told himself. "Spark" was a word that had special meaning in baseball.

A ball, hit by Poke, skimmed across the infield. Actually no game could have been less important—just six pick-ups to a team. But Hutch, following the ball intently, dove and missed. That grounder, skittering into the outfield, gave Poke a single and Hutch a fit.

The shortstop spanked the dirt from his trousers with a disgruntled look. "I give you Hutch Bannister," he said. "The All-American flop!"

Sleepy laughed. The ball had struck a rock—a bulldozer couldn't clear away everything—and no one, not even Buzz Kyler, could have fielded that grounder. But this was a fact that Sleepy saw where Hutch and Turkey didn't. On the pitcher's mound, Turkey scowled and made evident his belief that Hutch had let him down.

But that was Turkey's way. He was forever kicking the mound or bobbing his Adam's apple to show he felt sore when things didn't go right. And yet with a good curve and a slow, tantalizing slider, Turkey was a fine hurler. As if to prove this point, he whiffed fidgety, nearsighted Shad Rowe on three straight pitches.

"Next time I'll remember my glasses," Shad announced disgustedly.

Turkey said ungraciously, "Bring a pair of binoculars for all I care!"

At bat came blond, lanky Dodo Newson, whose sober, deacon-like face squinted in ferocious concentration. Dodo always seemed keyed-up, even when rummaging through ash cans in search of old stamps on envelopes to add to his collection, but Dodo could hit. On Turkey's first throw the lanky boy swung mightily and lifted a towering fly. Sleepy rushed back, grabbed the ball in the webbing of his glove, and saw Poke trapped between first and second.

"Take it, Hutch!" Sleepy cried, flinging the ball hard. Hutch caught it—otherwise the ball might have cut him in half—and Poke, notoriously a bad base runner, was out on the shortstop's frantic tag.

"Good playing," shouted Sleepy.

Turkey, who had run over to cover first and had been ignored, sniffed. "Good fielding, you mean. You could have outrun Poke to the bag had you wanted to!"

Sleepy nodded briefly. And he knew now why he disliked Turkey. What did he care about how Hutch might feel over a crack like that? Turkey's universe consisted of only one individual—Turkey Saunders, Esquire.

Sensing Sleepy's tight-lipped disapproval, Turkey grew defiant. "Who you tryin' to fool?" he asked as the teams changed sides. "You can play first an' Poke can catch an' I can pitch—maybe we've got six or seven fellows who are pretty good—but where would we get in the county league when a tight play depended on Hutch or Lover?"

"You can boot 'em too," Sleepy said shortly. Swinging two bats, he cast one aside and stepped up to the plate. On the mound now was Asphalt Smith, thin as a wire stretched between two telephone poles, who prided himself on his famous inshoot-outshoot that curved neither in nor out. Asphalt wasn't much of a pitcher. All Asphalt had on the ball was its cover, and Sleepy promptly drilled the first pitch where no pitch belonged—deep into the outer reaches of left field.

Turkey, going down to coach behind third where Sleepy

finally stopped, said, "We've got to face up to the truth. So we want a team in the Little League. Well, who's going to sponsor us?"

"Meaning what?" asked Sleepy, tagging the sack and dancing down toward home.

"To get into the Little League somebody's got to sponsor you. A team needs uniforms, bats, baseballs." Turkey shook his head. "It's quite a proposition. In Culver City it's the big cement company there who sponsors the Culver Mixers, and in Franklinville it's the rubber company who's behind the Franklin Firestones, but who would back a team—this kind of team—in little old Northfield?"

It was a mean question to ask a fellow leading down off third, or at least so Sleepy thought. When Tennessee Martin took Asphalt Smith's next futile inshoot-outshoot and lined it—as the harmless hermit thrush flies—into right field, Sleepy scampered home, glad to be free of Turkey's nagging pessimism.

The game staggered on, as pick-up games do, until it was time for lunch. Sleepy felt dejected. Basically everything Turkey said was true.

Shuffling along Maple Avenue, sunk in his own gloomy meditations, Sleepy was unaware of his father's approach until the man spoke over the boy's shoulder.

"What's this I hear about you kids wanting a team in the Little League?"

"Wantin' ain't gettin'," grumbled Sleepy.

"Your grammar, like your spirit, leaves much to be desired," Mr. Jones commented. "Now tell me the facts."

Sleepy told what he could about the bulldozer and the new ball field. A shrewd light came into Mr. Jones's eyes for when Sleepy described what it was like to play first on a good diamond excitement stole into his voice. But the boy ended on the same old worrisome note: "Still, there's no big cement or rubber company in Northfield."

"No, there isn't," Mr. Jones admitted. "Among all the businessmen of Northfield you won't find a real big shot. But as a group, we do all right, Sleepy. As a group, we try to keep Northfield the nice town it is. One of the reasons why we feel that way is because of kids like you. We want this to be your town, too."

"So why can't we have a ball team?"

"Have you thought of asking *all* the merchants that question?"

Sleepy stopped. "Would they back us?"

Mr. Jones smiled. "You'll never know," he said, "unless you ask!"

5 Monkey Business

SLEEPY'S HEAD throbbed with questions as he followed his father up the porch steps.

"Do you really think the merchants will sponsor us? How can we put it up to them? Will you go with me? Can we tackle some of them this afternoon when you close the store? Or early this evening?"

Across the screened doorway stood Sleepy's mother. She waited with legs parted and hands on hips, and in her cool blue eyes lurked a gleam of suspicion.

"What is this?" she asked. "*More* baseball?"

"Sure, it's more baseball," Sleepy replied aggressively. "Baseball's important!"

Mrs. Jones brushed back a wisp of stray hair from her forehead, and in the gesture a hint of increasing impatience could be detected.

"Baseball before breakfast," she said. "Baseball at lunch and supper and heaven only knows when else! Let me tell you, Sleepy Jones, things are going to be a bit different around here!"

Sleepy fell back on an old defense. "I should think you'd want a son and father to share common interests!"

Mrs. Jones accepted that challenge joyfully. "I do, Sleepy —believe me, I do! The common interest of keeping the grass mowed and the hedge trimmed, which you are going to do this afternoon. The common interest of a picnic with the family, on which you are going this evening. The common interest of sharing the delivery of orders at the store, on which you can begin tomorrow morning."

"I want more allowance," retorted Sleepy, who didn't surrender easily.

"So do I," said Mrs. Jones. "We'll both ask your father about it, and see who gets the first increase—judging, of course, on the basis of past performance!"

Sleepy wrinkled his nose. His mother's mood was not encouraging, but at times, Sleepy had learned, you gained more walking around a brick wall than trying to butt it down with your head. In the privacy of the living room, while Mrs. Jones retired to the kitchen to continue preparations for luncheon, Sleepy shifted the attack to his father.

"We shouldn't lose all this time," he said.

Mr. Jones put down his paper. "Sleepy," he replied, "did you ever hear of the 'balance of power'? Among nations, I mean. As long as enough nations, with enough strength, stand united behind the same basic principles they have a much better chance of maintaining world peace."

"Even if they gang up on a small nation that can't defend itself?"

"Even if they're mean enough to do that," Mr. Jones answered soberly. "Maybe it's tyranny or despotism or downright rotten or anything you want to call it, Sleepy, but that's how it is. And in this family as long as your mother and I stick together—even if we don't always agree with each other—we keep the 'balance of power.' It may not be fair, but it's effective!"

"It's a form of taxation without representation," avowed Sleepy.

"It's all of that," Mr. Jones agreed genially. "And dictatorship. But we enjoy it."

Overwhelmed by the conspiracy against him, Sleepy climbed the stairs to his room, but even here the despotic rule of his parents dogged him. Pinned to his unmade bed was a note:

> *Make this. Don't hang your clothes on the floor. Empty the wastebasket. Stop standing on your head when you read—or at least stop leaving books and old magazines under the desk. There is a broom in the hall closet.*

This ultimatum was signed:

> *By command of*
> *Your Terrible Mother,*
> *Officer-in-charge,*
> *The Jones Family.*

Sleepy sat down on the bed and started grinning. The note *was* funny. But, hang it, why did she have to pick today to think of the yard, or a doggone old picnic? There was, he tried to explain to his parents at lunch, a time and place for everything.

"Precisely," said Mrs. Jones. "Now's the time and the garage is the place where you'll find the lawn mower and the hedge clippers."

Mr. Jones chuckled. "Three strikes and you're out. Please pass the butter."

Sleepy, utterly defeated, thought that the butter tasted rancid.

"Maybe you've got a sour stomach," Mr. Jones suggested. "We'll skip the ice cream on the picnic."

Sleepy grimaced. This wasn't tyranny, but slavery.

After Sleepy had pushed the lawn mower once across the middle of the back yard, he looked behind him. The single swath of mowed lawn appeared neat and clean, but on both sides the uncut portions of grass loomed up like immense green jungles. Sleepy exhaled discouragedly.

A happy distraction, however, occurred at that moment. Up the driveway bounded Lover Carmichael, clad in green slacks and a green sweat shirt so that he looked like a thorn between two of the roses on which he once had orated to his everlasting fame.

"Hey, Sleepy," shrilled Lover, in his high, squeaky voice, "I've got the wire for the backstop! My Pop had a roll of it left over from building the fence around the dog kennels, and all we have to do is carry it over to the meadow."

"When?"

"Why not right now?"

Lover's enthusiasm and ambition touched Sleepy, the more so when he reflected that about the only position Lover could fill with competence on a Northfield team would be that of water boy. Still, Lover asked for no concessions. He simply wanted to do his part.

"Come on, huh, Sleepy? Let's you an' me fix up that backstop this afternoon!"

Sleepy, in a dismal gesture, extended his hand to indicate the uncut grass and the unclipped hedge. "I'm trapped," he said. "Orders from above."

"Darn!" groaned Lover. "I know. I get it in the neck, too!"

"They never can wait."

"You said it. Every morning I have to study spelling."

"In the *summer?*"

"In the summer," confessed Lover. "I flunked it in school."

The dominance of determined parenthood smote both boys. Sleepy leaned on the handle of the mower and scowled at the grass. In sympathy Lover jiggled a stone in his hand and also scowled at the grass.

"We'll get that backstop built," Lover muttered.

"Maybe tomorrow."

"I hope my pop doesn't forget before then and give that wire to someone else," said Lover, ignoring the fact that the same roll of wire had been stored in the Carmichael basement for the past two years.

Sleepy nodded.

"We better not wait too long," Lover went on darkly. "You never know. Gee—"

Lover broke off with the highest squeak he ever had managed. Never—not even in the "Red, red rose" part of a recitation—had Lover's eyes bulged more violently.

But Sleepy's own eyes bulged.

"Up there," piped Lover. "On the garage."

Sleepy blinked twice. "It's—it's—a—monkey!" he said in a hushed, awed voice.

Indeed, perched on the peak of the garage roof sat a monkey, calmly gazing down at the dumbstruck boys. The animal scratched itself nervously, and cocked its head to one side with a quick, obvious gesture of annoyance, as though to inquire angrily: "What's the matter with you lugs —haven't you ever seen a monkey before?"

At that moment a new excitement burst upon the Jones

backyard as two short and two long pairs of legs pounded up the driveway. This time Johnny Kyler's face seemed almost as red and sweat-larded as the face of his Irish friend, Kelly.

"We've found that devil Joanna," blustered the exhausted Kelly.

"Findin' her isn't catchin' her," flung back a panting Johnny.

The monkey, still scratching herself, stared down curiously at the new arrivals.

Between gulps for breath, Johnny told his story. Joanna was a twelve-year-old female Rhesus monkey that a Yankee fan had given Buzz for a pet. That morning, when the Kyler family had moved to Northfield, the monkey had been securely chained in the van. During the journey Joanna had worked out of her bonds and when they opened the van's door a ball of fur had hurtled over their heads.

"Ye should have seen that Joanna go!" exclaimed Kelly. "She must have flit through the air a good twenty-five foot!"

Lover said, "*Crickety!*" and Lover's high tone possibly irritated Joanna. Again she "flit"—straight over all their heads into the middle of the lawn. Once she looked back, apparently disliked what she saw, leaped the hedge—and was gone!

"After her!" shouted Johnny.

"Rascal—varmint—*flea-devil!*" bellowed Kelly, propelling himself back into motion.

The progression that soon spread out along Maple Avenue began to make Northfield history. First came Joanna, loping along with the speed of the wind, leaping small objects like bushes and parked cars, scampering along fences as though they had been constructed for her particular amusement, and, when the fancy struck her, seizing the limbs of trees and swinging herself forward in long, graceful bounds.

Johnny, Sleepy, and Lover dashed after Joanna, shouting and waving their arms, but they were no match for the galloping Rhesus, while Kelly, crimsoning like a sunset, brought up the rear in a burst of Irish petulence:

"Ye're killin' me, ye bloody wretches!"

But Kelly kept on running, doubtless fearing that when he stopped he would collapse forever.

"The traffic on Main Street will stop her," Sleepy panted hopefully.

Neither Johnny nor Lover dared spare the breath to fling back a reply.

Ahead stretched the corner of Maple Avenue and Main, where Padgett, the cop, directed traffic from under his awninged stand. Padgett was fat, and severe on jaywalkers, and not beyond losing the fine edge of his temper when events took the wrong turn. Also Padgett liked things to be orderly, as many a motorist had learned when he failed to keep his car within the white lines on the road.

But Joanna knew how to handle Padgett. With one leap she landed on top of the awninged stand, and it became difficult to tell who was directing traffic—Padgett or Joanna. Pedestrians shrieked. Two cars locked fenders. A third banged into a tree. And Padgett pulled out his club and shouted.

Kelly's Irish guile responded to the moment. "Boys, if ye'll take me advice, ye'll detour!"

Padgett, unflinching in the face of duty, revealed great resources of courage. With his club gripped between his teeth, he started to climb up on the awning. The stand tipped. Clearly Joanna felt that the policeman was too clumsy to be trusted. She moved.

Some said Joanna struck Padgett's head, then the top of the lamppost, and finally the seat of the hook-and-ladder standing in front of the firehouse. Others held to a second theory that Joanna made in one leap the distance from the awning to the seat. A third group, perhaps embellishing the facts, swore that they saw Joanna knock the club out of Padgett's mouth.

At any rate, the club dropped. So did Padgett. So did the stand. And so did Joanna from the seat of the hook-and-ladder. An alley dividing the firehouse from an adjoining building sensibly impressed Joanna as an appropriate avenue of escape.

"After her!" screamed Padgett.

"After her!" shouted Kelly, who knew when, as an innocent bystander, the moment had come to obey the law.

Johnny Kyler hung his head in shame.

"I guess," he said, "that Northfield will never forget the day when the Kyler family moved into town!"

6 Jumpin' Joanna

THE CULVER CITY PRESS, arriving in Northfield on the late afternoon train three days later, carried this headline on its front page. No one disputed the accuracy of the headline, and least of all Sleepy Jones, Lover Carmichael, Johnny Kyler, or the beleaguered Kelly. Inexhaustibly they had pursued Joanna, along with the enraged Padgett and such inhabitants of the town into whose neighborhood the chase had veered, and inexhaustibly Joanna had eluded all of them.

Actually, as the reporter from the *Press* pointed out, "eluded" was not a properly descriptive word. Joanna had been seen many times. Joanna, caught raiding Padgett's own vegetable garden, had been lassoed by that irate individual, but before Padgett could capture Joanna she had coolly slipped off the noose and "skeedaddled."

On another occasion Joanna had been surrounded in a tree. An ex-G. I. remembered that in Africa the soldiers had caught monkeys by dropping peanuts in a bottle. The monkeys, said the ex-G. I., pushed their paws into the bottle,

36

clutched the peanuts, and, too greedy to let go, couldn't pull their fists out of the bottle.

Under the ex-G. I.'s direction, a ripe banana was stuffed into a milk bottle, and raised by a pole so that it swung within Joanna's easy reach. The Rhesus stuck up her nose and seemed to say, "Who you kiddin'?"

"We'll get her with the blanket trick," promised Padgett resourcefully.

Under the policeman's direction, a blanket was spread on the ground and baited with the ripest, most succulent banana Northfield could provide. Ropes were tied to the four corners of the blanket and so rigged over the limbs of trees that at a shout from the officer the blanket could be snapped shut.

Padgett seized one rope and Kelly another, and Sleepy and Johnny were entrusted with the other ropes.

Joanna, interested, came down from the tree. She approached the blanket in a lazy, loping gait, sniffed, and crossed boldly after the bait.

Padget almost burst his lungs: *"Up!"*

Up went four pairs of arms, up went the blanket, and up went Joanna, climbing faster than any of them could pull. Up went the banana also—Joanna didn't risk her freedom for a pittance.

Kelly dropped his rope in disgust. "She's a match for all o' us!"

Buzz Kyler, joining the group, spoke sadly, "I suppose we could shoot her!"

Padgett's trigger finger clearly itched, but Sleepy felt stubborn. "If that's the way we get her we ought to be ashamed."

Buzz glanced around. He remembered Sleepy and the unhappy circumstances of their first meeting. The Yankees' former star spoke gratefully, "You're all right!"

Sleepy's heart glowed. After all, Buzz *had* hit that grand-slam home run. For that season at least, Buzz had been Mr. Baseball.

Meanwhile, on a branch of the tree Joanna finished the banana, threw the peeling at the assembled throng, and scampered away.

"In a way," said Mrs. Jones at supper that evening, "Joanna has changed all our lives. We never think or talk of much else."

With a grin Sleepy reflected that there had not been a renewal of the crusade to make him a victim of the "balance of power." He owed Joanna something!

"Why," continued Mrs. Jones, "we don't even hear about baseball any more!"

Mr. Jones chuckled. "I do," he said. "This Joanna business has made a laughingstock out of Northfield. In one way the publicity's amusing, but in another it has disadvantages. When you call a wholesaler for supplies you grow a little tired of being asked, 'Need any *monkey* wrenches?' So we merchants have been thinking that an investment in a little positive publicity might not be a bad idea."

Sleepy guessed he was dull-witted, for it took him a moment to realize what his father was saying. "You mean you're going to sponsor a Northfield team in the Little League?"

"I do."

"With uniforms and everything?"

"With all the fixin's."

"Well, holy cow!" exclaimed Sleepy. "Or I guess I should say, jumpin' Joanna!"

"I hope," said Mr. Jones, twinkling, "that you'll like the uniforms when you see them."

"Sure, we will! Say, what are they going to be like? Will Northfield be printed on them?"

"That," teased Mr. Jones, "is our secret."

Here was news that must be circulated, and Sleepy began gulping down the remainder of his supper. Surprisingly, Sleepy's mother appeared to understand the reason for his excitement and raised merely a mild objection. Why, Sleepy told himself, this news would rock the town! But there was one factor on which the boy did not reckon.

That was the evening Joanna selected to disport herself on the steeple of the Methodist Church.

Lover Carmichael burst into the Jones residence shouting, "They've got her, they've got her, *they've got her!*" When Lover could be persuaded to tone down his steam-whistle voice, he explained that where they "had" Joanna was cornered on the church steeple.

Mrs. Jones gathered up Mr. Trouble and said, "Come on, we're all going."

Within half an hour everyone in Northfield seemed to have the same notion. Even the reporter from the Culver City *Press* arrived.

Kelly's Irish spirits grew exuberant. "We'll get the fleabite this time!"

Johnny Kyler explained the plan. Buzz had conferred with a veterinarian and it had been decided to feed Joanna a banana drugged with sodium amytal so that she would go to sleep. After that, they'd climb up on ladders to the steeple and capture the Rhesus.

Dusk began to gather. Four searchlights, willingly brought

from police headquarters by the exasperated Padgett, held Joanna's figure in a blinding glare. Next the hook-and-ladder rumbled up and ladders were set in place on two sides of the steeple. Buzz and the veterinarian stood by stoically doping a banana with sodium amytal—with four times as much of the drug, Buzz declared, as should be necessary to put any twelve-year-old Rhesus to sleep for two weeks.

"It looks," said Sleepy a little sadly, "as though the jig is up for poor old Joanna."

Tenseness held the crowd below, said the reporter from the *Press*, like the tenseness that spreads through a town on Election Night or through the grandstand in the last inning of a hotly contested World Series game. Joanna, composed and dignified on the ledge of the steeple, looked down at her determined captors and yawned.

"She's a brazen one," growled Kelly. "The little hussy enjoys the limelight!"

Unquestionably, Joanna did. The monkey capered along the edge, showing off. Then as the drugged banana was raised toward her on a pole, she watched it greedily. She looked so hungry for the fruit that Lover swore he could feel the saliva rising in his own mouth.

The moment the banana came within reach, Joanna snatched it. The fruit disappeared down her gullet in an instant.

"Now we'll wait," announced Padgett with satisfaction.

"You know," Sleepy's father laughed, "Joanna makes me think of that old song about the bride whose groom didn't appear for the wedding—the one that goes:

> *And there was I*
> *Left waiting at the church,*
> *A-waiting at the church . . ."*

Joanna blinked in the glare of the searchlights.

"She's growing drowsy," Kelly predicted.

But Joanna wasn't growing drowsy. Instead, she acted bored and restless. Obviously there were to be no more bananas. Joanna's angry chattering suggested that a girl putting on as good a performance as hers deserved better treatment.

"I dunno," Sleepy said, "she looks awful lively to me."

Apparently the monkey also looked lively to Padgett, for the policeman said through gritted teeth, "She hasn't any sense of what's right!"

Joanna moved away from the ledge. She yawned. She covered her eyes against the lights. Then she yawned again.

Consumed by restlessness, Joanna uncovered her eyes and returned to the ledge. Once more the monkey looked down.

"Next she'll be having us croon *Rock-A-Bye-Baby,*" Kelly averred sarcastically.

Possibly Joanna feared that this indignity might be aimed at her. The legs of the Rhesus tensed and the next moment they saw her arching through the air. She caught hold of the limb of a tree, walked along the bough, and jumped again. The searchlights swung round desperately. Tree after tree shone in their penetrating glare.

But Joanna was gone!

"I can't believe it," yipped Lover.

"She beats me," Buzz groaned. "She had enough dope to make her sleep for two days. Maybe it had started to work, and that was why she lit out—because she began to feel funny!"

"Nobody's denying the old girl's intelligence," Mr. Jones said laughingly.

Sleepy assented with a chuckle.

Next day, across two columns, a front page headline in the Culver City *Press* declared:

JOANNA LEAVES 1,000 SUITORS
WAITING AT METHODIST CHURCH

7 *A Reluctant*
Recruit

THAT MORNING before breakfast Sleepy sat at his desk, composing an important document:

NORTHFIELD BASEBALL TEAM

1B—Sleepy Jones
2B—Tennessee Martin
3B—Asphalt Smith
SS—Hutch Bannister
LF—Dodo Newson
CF—Lover Carmichael
RF—Shad Rowe
C—Poke Johnson
P—Turkey Saunders

Many questions formed in Sleepy's mind while he labored over this line-up, and Hutch at shortstop loomed among the biggest. Hutch possessed the spirit, but could a fellow meet the measure of the Little League on spirit alone? Of course Asphalt would argue that his pitching ability was being wasted at third, but Asphalt might as well argue that the man in the moon was Turkey's great-grandfather! When Sleepy's glance rested on his selection for centerfield sadness filled his reflections. Nothing but sheer desperation warranted putting Lover anywhere in the outfield! Still, who else was there?

This final query, which should have deprived Sleepy of the last remnants of his appetite, produced quite an opposite result. There *was* someone else—Johnny Kyler! If anyone should know baseball it should be the son of the famous Buzz! And Johnny could run—that much he had demonstrated the first time they all had chased after Joanna.

"Chances are, he's better than any of us," Sleepy muttered. "We can put Johnny at short and Hutch in center." As for poor old Lover, he could be team manager—a fancy name for water boy. Johnny made the difference all right, giving Northfield a good infield and sending out Hutch to plug the weakness in center. Darn if the Little League wouldn't soon discover that there was something besides Joanna that made Northfield newsworthy!

But Joanna remained a problem. When the team Sleepy had picked gathered at the meadow for practice, Lover expressed the undercurrent of restlessness.

"Hang it, but it seems we ought to catch that pesky monkey first!"

"One thing is sure," Asphalt said, "we won't see Johnny around here until Joanna *is* caught."

Sleepy scowled at the ground. What Asphalt suspected was probably all too true.

Poke spoke tentatively. "Couldn't we build a trap to bag her?"

"With what?" Asphalt demanded.

"Why, with that roll of wire Lover's dad is giving us for

the backstop. After the trap works, we can tear it down and use the wire for the backstop."

The trap—officially named Poke's Pipe Dream in honor of its creator—became a work of art. A circular space about six feet in diameter was wired off, with heavy stakes driven into the ground to make the base secure. Next wire was laced over the top so that Joanna couldn't leap out of the stockade. The trap door, really the invention of Tennessee Martin, displayed the kind of mind that built prisons like a Bastille or a San Quentin. A weight from a window sash gave the door ballast so that once it slammed it would stay shut.

"See how it'll work?" Tennessee asked, first sliding the door up and down between the poles he had fashioned for a frame. "It's held up by the delicate balance of this stick, on which we hang the bananas we want Joanna to grab. See, a slight touch—out goes the stick—and down comes the door!"

"With Joanna sealed up inside," cried Asphalt in admiration.

But Lover thought of one more embellishment. A rope was tied to the door and fastened on the other end to a cowbell.

"So down goes the door," exclaimed Lover. "Clang goes the bell. One of us will hear it for sure and we can come a-runnin' before Joanna tears her way out of this booby-hatch!"

Word of the building of the trap spread quickly, and among those who appeared to examine the gang's handiwork were Johnny and Kelly. The location of the snare on the much-traveled footpath from Maple Avenue to the meadow was judged an excellent choice. And Lover's addition of the cowbell earned many compliments.

"Ye've done yerselves proud," conceded Kelly. "An' if anybody's mind should work like a monkey's 'twould be the mind o' a boy!"

Poke chuckled. "Ordinarily Padgett would raise hob with us for closing off what amounts to a public thoroughfare, but in this case I bet he'll close one eye."

"Aye, there ye have a point," agreed Kelly.

To Sleepy the congenial spirit of the moment suggested that this was a good time to approach Johnny about the team.

"You've got to come out!"

Johnny scuffled a foot in the grass. "I'm pretty new around here."

"We need you, Johnny."

"Some of the others may object."

"Object, my hat! It's what's good for the team that counts."

Johnny seemed to perspire prodigiously. "I—I'm not very good at baseball," he blurted.

Sleepy wouldn't believe him. The son of Buzz Kyler had to play a fair game of baseball—better, anyhow, than the sort of butterfinger performance that distinguished Lover's playing.

"All right," Johnny said. "I'll get my glove. There's one way to cure this nonsense. Seeing is believing."

In the hour remaining before lunch, another pick-up game was organized. With Asphalt pitching, Sleepy played first and instructed Johnny to cover second. Shad Rowe, this time remembering to bring his glasses, played in left field and Lover in right.

Asphalt's inshoot-outshoot proved no more effective than it ever had. Turkey, first to come up, was the weakest batsman of the group; but even Turkey could hit Asphalt's offerings, and rapped a hard grounder past the mound.

Sleepy watched Johnny chase after the ball. His glove reached out. And then Johnny stumbled in his awkward anxiety and the ball bounded off his foot into the outfield.

By the time Lover had galloped after the ball, fumbled it, and finally thrown to a screeching Sleepy, Turkey rested safely on third.

Johnny's face burned with shame. Grim-lipped, he walked back to his position at second. And at last Sleepy's great faith that all members of the Kyler clan were natural baseball players wavered.

In the long, agonizing minutes that followed this faith was shattered completely. Johnny did nothing right. He overran hits and booted them with his feet. When the ball did connect with his glove there seemed to be a spring hidden in the padding that bounced the ball back into the air. Everyone managed to steal against Johnny and there was no sense throwing the ball for that was only inviting the runner to take still another base while Johnny bobbled the ball or appeared to be playing marbles with it on the edge of the infield grass.

At first Turkey and Poke hooted, but their derision soon was silenced. Anybody could see that Johnny suffered miserably. The redness that at first had burned only in his cheeks reached now to the roots of his damp, blond hair. His glance remained fixed on the ground as though he found the dirt around the base more comforting to contemplate than Sleepy's astonished gaze. Turkey and his teammates had scored six runs. There were no outs.

Johnny slammed his glove on the ground and faced Sleepy. "I hope you're satisfied!"

"It's only a practice game," Sleepy murmured weakly.

Johnny's tortured emotions exploded at Sleepy's silly comment.

"I hate baseball," he cried. "If you want my opinion, baseball's a game for dumb clucks!"

Johnny snatched his glove from the ground and stuffed it into his back pocket. Then, struggling against the tears that stung his eyes, he turned sharply and stomped off toward home.

Sleepy watched the hunched, humiliated figure striding across the field. The old meadow was unnaturally quiet.

"I think," Turkey began, and then stopped.

What could anyone say?

Sleepy kicked at first base. He had been a fool, insisting that Johnny come out for the team, too stupid to understand what Buzz's son had tried to tell him. He had hurt Johnny unnecessarily, a mucker's trick.

Lover sighed, "Gee!" The word came out in a forlorn, protracted squeal. For that morning, at any rate, the fun had gone out of baseball!

Clang!

Sleepy's head bobbed up.

Clang! Clang!

The tolling of the cowbell rolled lustily across the meadow.

"Joanna's sprung her trap!" bellowed Tennessee in giddy relief.

Bats, balls, gloves were left scattered on the diamond as the boys leaped forward. Hutch reached the footpath first. If Hutch had paused a single stride a dozen comrades would have whizzed over him.

But then Hutch did stop, and so did all his companions. There sat Joanna, on *top* of the trap, looking extremely indignant. Inside the trap with the door closed sat Sleepy's three-year-old brother, Mr. Trouble, calmly eating the banana.

"Good! *Good!*" announced Mr. Trouble to his speechless audience. He continued shoving the banana into his mouth.

Joanna, convinced that she was to be deprived of any share in the fare, jumped up and down in a rage. Then, clutching the branch of a tree, she swung over the cage and snarled at the boy below.

Mr. Trouble ate on, undisturbed.

Joanna dropped to the ground and indignantly circled the cage. Then she stopped, seized the chicken-wire sides of the enclosure in her front paws and shook them furiously. Mr. Trouble finished the banana and neatly folded the peel.

"Eat! *Eat!*" he invited Joanna, shoving the skin in her direction.

Joanna had borne the last insult she could endure. With a final hiss at Mr. Trouble the Rhesus hopped around and disappeared through the bushes. At every stride she chattered with mounting displeasure—like a fussy old lady on a bus who is sure the driver has shortchanged her, Poke said afterward.

But now Sleepy spoke first.

"If this hasn't been the doggonedest morning for things to go backward!"

8 Order Out
of Chaos

"WE'LL really have to do something about that monkey," Sleepy's mother insisted. "Goodness only knows what she may do next to poor Mr. Trouble!"

"You mean it's anybody's guess what Mr. Trouble may do to poor Joanna," Sleepy corrected.

Mr. Jones laughed. "In this case, I think Sleepy's right!"

Throughout the family's discussion Mr. Trouble amused himself by unlacing Sleepy's first baseman's glove. Sleepy's morning already had been sufficiently upset by Johnny Kyler *and* Joanna *and* all the work and time that had gone into building the useless trap. The older boy snatched up the glove and calculated what the cost might be if he used it to clout Mr. Trouble's head.

The doorbell rang. Sleepy's father answered and Sleepy heard him ask, "Won't you come in, Mr. Kyler?"

Buzz sat on the sofa in the living room, self-consciously fingering the brim of his hat. From watching close-ups on television of big league players, Sleepy had learned that in tense moments they all acquired fidgety habits.

"I'm glad your little boy wasn't hurt," Buzz said.

"We were just saying that's how we felt about Joanna," Mr. Jones replied with a smile.

"I guess we'll have to end this nonsense by shooting that fool Rhesus," Buzz said sadly.

Mr. Trouble became intrigued by this suggestion and dashed across the room screaming, "Shoot! Shoot!"

"Do you mind if I sit on his stomach to keep him quiet?" Sleepy asked sourly.

The two men grinned.

"Buzz, we're glad you moved to Northfield," Mr. Jones said. "It's nice to have you and your family—and even Joanna. We hope you'll find time soon to come to one of the meetings of our Businessmen's Luncheon Club."

"I'd like that very much," Buzz replied. "I want to take an active role in town affairs."

Sleepy could have sworn that from across the room his father winked at him.

"Then I think," Mr. Jones told Buzz, "that we have just the job for you."

"I'll be glad to do anything."

"Fine. And this job should be easy. The boys need a coach for the team they're entering in the county's new Little League."

In much the same way that the old meadow had grown quiet when Johnny Kyler had stalked home from the practice game, a stillness crept into the Jones living room. Sleepy's heart might almost have skipped a beat if he had not been absorbed by the strained look that filled Buzz's face. When

Johnny had glanced down at Sleepy from the bulldozer that day in the meadow, the same remote, unfathomable expression had been in the boy's countenance. The Yankee's once-great star stared down at the rug when he spoke.

"I had told myself that I didn't especially like baseball any more, Mr. Jones."

"You can't expect a bunch of normal, healthy boys to understand an attitude like that, Buzz."

Buzz Kyler smiled crookedly. "Yeah, when I was a kid—"

"What would it have meant then if somebody like you had come along and offered to coach the gang?"

Silence returned to the living room, and Buzz's fingers, toying with the brim of the hat, beat an unconscious tattoo. Then, gradually, the crookedness disappeared from his smile.

"All right, Mr. Jones," he said, "I'll coach the team. From three to five in the afternoon. Starting tomorrow."

When Buzz stood up his glance fell on Sleepy. "What position do you play?"

"First base."

"Well, on this team you're going to be the best first baseman in the county!"

Sleepy moved off into a world part real, part dream. With Buzz for a coach, a fellow who didn't make the grade had only himself to blame. But the wonder that filled Sleepy wasn't for this fact alone. Sure, Buzz would bring order out of chaos and give them a real team—that was certain.

"But look at my dad," Sleepy thought. "All he's ever done is run a dinky hardware store in a dinky town like this. Seventy thousand people never jumped up at once to cheer him. And yet he got Buzz to do what he wanted—when Buzz really didn't want to do it—just as easy as though he were selling him a pound of nails!"

Sleepy walked into the yard, proud and happy. It wasn't any secret, either, why Buzz had come around. He had respected Sleepy's father.

An hour later Mrs. Jones, coming out into the yard, stopped short.

"Sleepy," she said, "are you willingly, voluntarily, under no duress or coercion, actually clipping the hedge?"

"Uh-huh."

"No bribe from your father?"

"Nope."

"No misdeed you've been up to so that this will ease the blow?"

Sleepy put down the hedge clippers. "Mom," he asked, "why are you such a suspicious woman?"

Mrs. Jones sighed. "I don't know, Sleepy. Honestly I don't —unless I've lived around boys too long!"

That night for supper they had apricot pudding, one of Sleepy's favorite desserts.

Afterward, lounging in the porch hammock, which was Sleepy's pet loafing spot, something seemed wrong. The book Sleepy had been reading—a rousing adventure story—couldn't be at fault for the restlessness that kept nipping at the boy. Only a guilty conscience ever troubled a fellow like this. And how would he feel if somebody had forced him to make a fool of himself the way he had made a fool of Johnny Kyler? He'd want to mope for a month unless somebody helped to stir him out of the blue funk he'd be in. Resolutely, Sleepy abandoned the book and the comfort of the hammock.

Mr. Jones looked up from the evening paper. "Getting kind of late to be buzzing off, isn't it, Sleepy?"

"Yes and no—I mean, I think this matter is important enough."

"Back soon?"

"About an hour."

Mr. Jones nodded. "I'll tell your mother, but don't be any later. She'll worry."

The home into which the Kylers had moved was on Locust Street, about a block off Maple—a big, rambling old house with plenty of yard around it. Last year the property had been the Whitmore place, and Sleepy remembered it best for the arbors in the back that toward late summer were loaded with Concord grapes. The Whitmores always had allowed the boys to eat all they wanted—after all, they couldn't be any worse vandals than the sparrows or starlings or peewees—and curious to see how the crop was coming this year, Sleepy cut across the grass toward the arbors.

Voices caught Sleepy's attention. They were familiar voices, tensed and low-pitched.

Johnny said, "Some day I'll go back an' show 'em!"

"Ye'll kill me doin' it!" complained Kelly. "Use yer knee, lad. Get it down in front o' the ball so it can't go through yer legs!"

"What—my knee!"

"No, the ball, an' don't be takin' me literally. Now, go after it!"

Kelly threw the ball and Johnny trapped it between his glove and his leg.

"That's a mite better. But get yer glove in front o' ye. Here, throw the ball to me."

When the ball came bounding back, Kelly gloved it

easily. Kelly was good. But Kelly was old and hot and growing tired. "First 'tis up before breakfast with the bulldozer, then chasin' that Joanna, an' now 'tis Honus Wagner ye'd have me be. Here, knuckle into it!"

Johnny's catch was the best that Sleepy had seen him make all day. "But gosh," Sleepy thought, "this is no spot for me!" The session under the arbor was strictly Johnny's private affair—and Kelly's.

Sleepy turned to retrace his way homeward when he realized that he was not the only silent observer to the scene under the arbor. Buzz walked over and joined Sleepy; together they recrossed the yard as far as the sidewalk on Locust Street.

"He's not much good," Buzz said. "When I should have been teaching him how to play I thought that I didn't have the time."

"Kelly's really helping him."

"Kelly, I guess, is a better father to Johnny than I am." The comment was so softly uttered that Sleepy couldn't believe he was supposed to have heard it. Buzz forced a smile then, and said in a firmer voice, "See you tomorrow, Sleepy. And get to bed early. That's a cardinal rule when you're in training."

Sleepy walked up Locust to Maple, shaking his head. There was something screwy about the Kylers that he couldn't quite figure out.

At the corner of Maple the inexhaustible Padgett appeared. He was searching diligently under all the bushes.

"Looking for your girl friend Joanna?" Sleepy chuckled.

Padgett's body snapped erect.

"Young Mr. Jones," he said, " 'tis not for you to sass the Law, and 'tis not a thing that would have happened before that confounded Joanna came here. Now I say to you, young Mr. Jones, what I said to my Missus this evening. That monkey Joanna has begun to demoralize the entire town."

A large wad of paper protruded from Padgett's back pocket, and, impishly, Sleepy wondered if it could be a warrant for Joanna's arrest. Wisely, however, the boy refrained from any observation on the subject.

9 With No
Punches Pulled

IF SOMEONE had pinned two well boiled beets to the sides of Lover Carmichael's head in place of the ears that were normally there, these portions of Lover's anatomy could not have looked more conspicuous.

Lover had just laid down a bunt and now waddled along the base path toward first with the motion of an animated wheelbarrow. Behind him bounced Buzz Kyler, cutting the afternoon air with a torrent of abuse.

"Lover, give me those daisies, please!"

Little Lover squeaked piteously, "What daisies?"

"Why, that bunch of daisies you must have stopped to pick when you were supposed to *run* for first!" Buzz looked the way he sounded—mad. "Lover, what kind of baseball is that? You looked to see whether that bunt would roll fair or foul *before* you started running. Of course you were thrown out by ten feet—you gave that much distance before you started. Now you get back there and bunt again. You let the umpire worry over where that ball's going. Once your bat hits that ball you light out of that batter's box—pronto,

57

just as though Joanna had her teeth in the seat of your trousers!"

In a pair of old baseball pants that doubtless were a relic of Buzz's days with the New York Yankees, the new Northfield coach revealed no sympathy as a dejected Lover trotted back to the plate.

Sleepy didn't know whether to grin or to feel sorry. The first hour of practice under Buzz had passed, and a bristling, tough-headed hour it had proved! One thing you could say for Buzz. He pulled no punches. He played no favorites.

Asphalt, toiling on the mound for the second half of the practice, pitched hard. Lover's bat went up. The ball trickled across the infield. Little Lover fled for first as though all the demons of mythology nipped at his heels. The ball came across the field and Sleepy reached out to scoop in the throw.

"Don't let that Jones ape block you off the base!" Buzz roared. "Plow right into him!"

But Lover, who would walk eight blocks out of his way to avoid an argument, hesitated, and by that step was thrown out.

Buzz kicked the ground.

"Look, Lover, do you know what you do? You flunk at baseball just the way you flunk at spelling!"

Lover's eyes flew open. How did Buzz know about his spelling?

"If you're going to coach a fellow," snapped Buzz, "you've got to know all you can about him. Baseball isn't something you add to a man. It's something already in him that has to come out! And you, my little Love Bird, like to spare yourself. You're mushy—like tapioca pudding. But you're going to get over it—right now! Go back and bunt again!"

Lover's tongue seemed to hang out—he was that hot and

"No alibis!" Buzz answered shortly.

tired. He returned to the plate with his eyes smoldering. A new feeling was rising in Lover—a feeling he never before had experienced—the feeling that if Sleepy got in his way he *could* dump him. Lover was afraid to explore too deeply into this new emotion, or else he might revert to the same old second-fiddle complex that had dogged him all his life. Asphalt unlimbered, the ball came in, Lover's bat went up, and then his spikes flashed along the base path.

Sleepy saw Lover charging down, jaw set, eyes snapping— an awesome sight.

Buzz bellowed, "If he blocks you, Lover, give him the old heave-ho!"

Lover looked as though he could run through a brick wall. Sleepy set himself for the throw as Asphalt scrambled after the bunt. But Sleepy was careful to give Lover's pounding spikes a clean path. Lover crossed the bag ahead of the ball.

"Well," sighed Buzz, standing over Sleepy, "where were you?"

"I—I—"

"You pulled back. You gave the runner an extra step. You're some first baseman!"

Sleepy said, "You want me to bounce him on his neck?"

"Only if you have to. Baseball isn't murder. But you play that bag. Do you see it? That square thing! It's spiked to the ground. And it's yours. Sit on it, sleep on it, do anything— but keep it all covered!"

Sleepy felt his temper rising, but when he looked up, there was no hostility in Buzz's glance. The man's quiet manner said, "Now you be reasonable, Sleepy—you know I'm only stating a fact."

Lover, keeping close to the base, looked elated. Sleepy watched him, wonderingly. Maybe this darn squeaky-voiced kid could make a fair player! And there was one thing you had to admit with Buzz. Maybe there was a sting in his voice when he lashed out, but you knew you'd soon have company in your misery. Buzz saw everything that went wrong. No one was spared.

Just then a batted ball took a bad bounce and glanced off Hutch's shoulder. Intuitively Hutch began to rub the tender spot, and Buzz stormed across the infield:

"Get that ball! Always field the ball before you worry over where you're hurt!"

"I suppose if the ball knocks my head off I just let it roll," Hutch flung back, peeved.

"Exactly!" Buzz told him coldly. "The head wouldn't do you much good and the ump wouldn't let you use it to tag the runner!"

Buzz, however, examined Hutch's shoulder and massaged it gently. "There are darn few whacks in baseball you can't rub out," he said, the bite gone out of his tone. "Only don't give the hitter an extra base doing it. Extra bases cost ball games and that may hurt worse than the sock on your skin!"

Hutch appeared mollified.

Sleepy suspected that when the first day's practice ended there would be two attitudes toward Buzz. If you wanted to take his criticisms personally then you could decide that you understood why Joanna, once she escaped, clung so tenaciously to her freedom. Or you could see that Buzz only pressed you to do your best and that nothing else would ever satisfy him. Sure, Buzz was a driver, but he'd give 'em a team —if they could take it!

One thing, anyhow, was certain. Lover had been reborn. Sleepy recognized the transformation in the goofy way Lover stuck out his chest. When Sleepy was called in to bat, Lover, who had scored on the last hit and returned to the bench, spoke as though his berth on the team was assured.

"We'll go somewhere with Buzz. We'll be quite a team!"

Wait, thought Sleepy, until you muff one of those flies!

But Buzz wasn't worrying about his outfield that first day. He didn't care too much about previous playing performance, he said. Over and over he returned to the same theme: "You play baseball with what you've got in your heart. A fighting heart makes a fighting player. To be good you've got to *want* to be good, then *work* to be good!"

Dirt streaked Buzz's sweaty face. No one could say he was afraid to work.

"He's all right," Lover said, filled with admiration.

Before Sleepy could answer, Buzz called him to the plate.

"Just swing," the coach said, "and let me watch."

Sleepy connected cleanly.

"A natural swing," Buzz admitted, "but straighten out that elbow."

Sleepy swung and missed.

"You know why?"

"I tried too hard."

"Not at all. You can't really try too hard. You were watching your elbow and not the ball. This time get it right!"

For five minutes Sleepy swung. Buzz never let up: "Elbow straighter—*elbow straighter!*" Sleepy expected to hear that insistent, merciless voice in his slumbers. But then he connected solidly. The ball took off on a line, lifting over the infield—lifting, lifting.

"How'd you like that?" Buzz asked.

"It was fine."

"Well, try to remember it. Turkey next."

At best Turkey Saunders was only a fair hitter. "Like most pitchers," he explained to Buzz.

"No alibis in advance, thank you!" Buzz answered shortly.

Turkey missed the first pitch. Then the second. Buzz stepped over to a tree and drew a mark on the bark. The team gathered around.

"Hit it," Buzz told Turkey.

Turkey's bat struck the tree inches away from the mark.

"You don't look at what you're doing," Buzz said stoically. "You keep swinging till you hit that mark three times straight."

Turkey's Adam's apple began bobbing. The tree trunk had a spring that made the bat sting. Moreover, this wasn't Turkey's idea of how he wanted to play baseball, an opinion that he made manifest by the lessening enthusiasm he put behind each swing. Behind him Buzz chanted heartlessly: "Missed again—*missed again*—MISSED AGAIN!"

Tennessee Martin, Poke Johnson, and Shad Rowe couldn't resist the chance to tease the easily flustered Turkey.

"Choppin' wood, Turk?"

"Better oil that rusty gate!"

"Mighty Casey had struck out!"

The Adam's apple flew up and down and the lines around Turkey's mouth grew tight. All at once he flung down the bat.

"I've had enough," he announced.

"You weren't trying," Buzz retorted quietly.

Turkey lost his head. "Is—is this the kind of stuff that made Johnny such a big-shot ball player?"

No one said anything. Turkey looked scared, but tried to

conceal his alarm behind a defiantly stuck-out chin. Buzz's eyes narrowed. Then, his voice very low, he said:

"That's all for today. If you like, Turkey, you can come over to my house after supper and apologize. Otherwise you're off the team!"

Lover said, walking back along Maple Avenue with Sleepy, "Do you think Buzz meant it?"

"I'm afraid he'll have to mean it," Sleepy grumbled. "After all, everyone heard him say it!"

"But Turkey's our best pitcher!"

"Our only pitcher!"

Lover pulled up a handful of grass and chewed it to hide his unhappiness. "If Turkey gets stubborn it'll spoil everything!"

"I think Turkey will apologize," Sleepy said thoughtfully, "but he still may leave things pretty blamed unsettled."

"I don't see that."

"It's Turkey. He'll hold onto a grudge. He's that way."

Lover returned to his grass chewing.

Sleepy learned after supper that Turkey had apologized—not very gracefully, but convincingly enough so that Buzz had capitulated.

Kelly was Sleepy's confidant. A restlessness that drove Sleepy to find out the truth about Johnny if he could led the boy to the little cottage across from the railroad station that the Irishman had rented.

"Here's where I hang me hat," said Kelly. "An' wonder what new deviltry Joanna's up to. A lone monkey, me lad, receives more attention than a lone old man."

"Kelly, is Johnny coming out for the team?"

"Mebbe."

"He and Buzz seem a strange pair!"

About to light his pipe, the Irishman held the match above the bowl and studied Sleepy's face. "An' what could ye mean by that?"

"Well, maybe nothing."

The fireflies were thick in the hedges across by the railroad station. Kelly watched them for a time, smoking quietly. Just when Sleepy had decided that the Irishman had forgotten his presence the man said, "If ye've got a moment, lad, I'll tell ye a story."

10 Kelly's Story

"SURE," SLEEPY said. "I'd be glad to hear it, Kelly."

The Irishman smiled.

" 'Tis a polite boy ye are, Sleepy, an' I hope ye'll like me story, laddie, for it begins, as most Irish stories do, with a whoppin' big lie.

"Ye see, I was never a boy in the sense ye know. Really I was—in me heart, for that's never grown old. I was just born simple-minded, ye might say, an' I've gone on bein' simple-minded, which is a good thing or a bad thing, dependin' on whether ye're Irish or English.

"Very early in me life me father died. He was a poor, unhappy man who took the hard knocks o' livin' as a personal feud 'tween him an' the devil. He was, as some fool Irishmen are, a man o' prodigious drinkin' habits, an' one night when he had swilled too much he walked off a dock an' drowned himself, as only a fool Irishman could.

"So there was me dear old Mother left with more children on her hands than she ever could provide for, an' the only way out was to parcel us off among her relations wherever she could find a taker. An uncle in America drew me—all he ever won in an Irish sweepstakes, he used to say—an' he gave me a bed an' found me a job an' I had no more complaints than befits an Irishman, which is to complain about everything.

"So I was young an' old all at once, ye might say. Not much schoolin'—too busy for that. Not ever married—the right girls got the habit o' lookin' the wrong way. But I got along, sometimes on a piece o' cheese like a churchmouse, an' then one day I got the lucky break that the good Lord keeps 'specially for the Irish."

Old Kelly paused to suck vigorously on his pipe to start it smoking once more, and Sleepy watched the fireflies lighting up the hedges across by the railroad station.

"'Twas six or seven years ago when it happened," the man resumed presently. "At the time I was drivin' a taxi in New York. Well, one day I'm cruisin' along lookin' for a fare when a young man darts out beside me cab an' starts hoppin' around as though his britches were on fire!

"'Quick,' says he, 'ye've got to get me to the Yankee Stadium!'

"That season there was a hot series on with the Boston Red Sox an' the whole town was het up over how the American League lead kept switchin' from day to day 'twixt the Yanks an' those boys from Bean-town.

"'I'm Buzz Kyler,' says the young man with all the impudence in the world. 'I guess ye know who I am.'

"'I'm Patrick Kelly,' I says, 'an' please to meet ye, an' now if ye don't mind just who are ye?'

"Well, that took a tuck in him. Ye could see he was cocky, an' felt important like a pouter pigeon, an' he didn't think I was serious. So again he told me his name. 'I play with the Yankees,' he says. 'Yesterday I hit the two doubles that won the game!'

" 'Sorry,' I says, 'for not recognizin' ye, Mr. Kyler, but I'm just a dumb Mick who doesn't keep up as I should with ye professional shillelagh-swingers, but if ye want to get to the Stadium fast I'm the boy who can get ye there!'

"Ye see, I was verra good at judgin' the traffic lights an' knew when to turn a corner to duck a red one here or pick up a green one there an' this Buzz rocked back and forth as we weaved our way through that clutter o' traffic with scarce a stop.

" 'Ye're all right,' he says.

" 'If a Kelly is good for anything,' I tells him, ' 'tis for chasin' after the devil.'

"He laughs an' says, 'Meet me at the Stadium after the game an' I'll give ye a fare back.' So I did, an' then, whenever the Yankees were in town, I'd take him to the games an' wait for him afterward, an' by an' by we'd grown to be pretty thick friends."

A freight train rumbled along the track and Kelly waited for the noise of the rattling cars to fade away. Sleepy read the names of a dozen railroads on the sides of the boxcars and thought how strange it was that something that had happened years ago—or hundreds of miles away—suddenly entered your life and perhaps changed everything.

"I liked Buzz a lot," Kelly went on, "but I could tell there was some great unsettlement on his mind. As the sayin' goes, he was the toast o' the town, for when he was hittin' the Yankees was winnin' an' sometimes the kids—an' the grownups, too—would be lined up for a block waitin' for his autograph. Wherever he went, folks seemed to know him. He was as well known as, in the old country, ye'd expect a horse thief to be.

"He pretended not to like all this attention, but he loved it, an' bein' Irish meself an' therefore a bit on the fickle side I pretended 'twas all an annoyance to me too but I always managed to get him to the Stadium when the crowd waitin' for him would be the largest. An' once when Buzz couldn't sign a fan's score card 'cause he was pressed to get to the dressin' room I signed the card meself: 'Patrick Kelly, chauffeur to Buzz Kyler.' Well, I thought Buzz would laugh for a week, he was so pleased. An' after that, I'd say, we were a bit cosier.

"So one day I says, 'Underneath there's something eatin' ye, an' as an old friend I can see it, an' I think ye better bring it out in the open where we both can take a boot at it!'

"'Twas funny the way he acted, lookin' first at the floor an' then out the window—anywhere 'cept at me. But he says all at once, 'Kelly, how'd ye like a new job?'

"'Mr. Kyler,' I says, 'I'm a mite old to become bat boy of the Yankees.'

"He smiled. 'I was thinkin',' he says, 'that ye might like to become a companion for my son.'

"Well, it all came out then about Johnny. His mother, it seems, had suffered a stroke an' was a bedridden invalid. An' baseball took Buzz around the league, or South for spring trainin', or off to Mexico an' South America playin' exhibition games in the off season, an' he wasn't much o' a father.

"'The kid doesn't get a break,' he says.

"When I met this Johnny for the first time, I was surprised. I thought he'd be a wet smack, but he was nice as could be 'cause even if his mother couldn't be around him too much she could teach him good manners. But he was lonely. I could sense it as Buzz had. An' so I took the job.

"Now, Sleepy, me lad," old Kelly said, "'tis not easy for a boy to have a famous father. In many ways, 'tis a handicap. Take Johnny an' baseball. Right at the start, I'd try to get him to play but he was never more than half-hearted at the idea. Buzz was the ball player in the family, Johnny insisted, an' all he could ever be was a ham by comparison. Actually he was afraid o' the game 'cause Buzz was so good —afraid, ye see, that he would fail by his father's standards. So he decided not to try at all.

"Still, Johnny loved baseball. I could tell by all the scrapbooks he kept filled with clippings about his dad, an' by the way he'd cheer when we went to a game at the Stadium. Then one day Buzz sprained his back, as ye may or may not know . . ."

Kelly paused. The shadows were much thicker, and the glow of the pipe bowl tinged the air with a reddish light.

"In professional baseball," said Kelly, "ye can go up fast but ye can come down faster. An' so it was with Buzz. One season he was the pride o' the Yankees an' the next he was back kickin' around the minors. Eatin' in cheap hotels. Ridin' on busses. Fightin' that pain in his back an' not gettin' any better.

"Just one game I took Johnny to after Buzz began sinkin' down that minor league toboggan. I wish now we'd never gone, for Johnny found a new fear that night o' what failure can mean in a high-strung sport like baseball.

"Poor old Buzz had nothin' that game except his physical misery. He fanned twice an' with the bases loaded the best he could do was hit into a double play. Once he misjudged a fly an' it got by him for a three-bagger. The fans hooted an' booed. Ye couldn't blame 'em. They'd paid their money to see a star, not a has-been. Buzz, he just grinned—he was a pro seein' the end of his career an' takin' it with his chin up.

"But Johnny only thought of the Buzz who had been—of the great hero who had died right before his eyes. He couldn't keep the tears from rollin' down his face. When I drove him home, he pressed his head against me an' sobbed all the way.

"So when ye ask me, Sleepy, if Johnny's comin' out for the team I have to think o' all this an' tell ye, in the confidence o' man to man, that I don't know. I wish he would 'cause I think the boy should lick that fear o' himself an' that fear o' failin' in front o' Buzz. An' he need not be a bad player—in the right spot. So we'll have to see. Sometimes a wound like that heals an' sometimes it doesn't."

Sleepy wondered how he would feel if he had to watch his father being booed as Buzz had been. Suddenly he felt choked up, and wished that he were home. Now that he knew the secret of the old meadow, he thought that it might be better if he didn't.

Dusk began to settle thickly; it would soon be dark. Beside the boy Kelly stirred.

"I'll walk along with ye a way," the old Irishman offered.

"You needn't, if it's a bother."

" 'Tis not, me lad. After all, I've nothing much to do. An', who knows, mebbe I'll come upon that Joanna!"

Happily Kelly's reference to the Rhesus monkey eased the tension.

"You'd think she'd have been caught by now!" Sleepy exclaimed.

"She's been seen by lots o' people, an' she even came close enough to one lady to take a potato chip out o' the woman's hand, but that's as near as anybody gets to puttin' Joanna back on that chain!" Kelly knocked his pipe against a tree trunk, and kicked thoughtfully at the last embers. "Still, me lad, there must be a way o' capturin' that Rhesus!"

A note of suppressed excitement ran through Kelly's voice.

"You've got a plan!" Sleepy guessed.

"An' have I now?" The Irishman laughed. "Well, if I have —an' I'm not sayin' yes or no—I'm keepin' it to meself."

"Aw, Kelly—"

"No, Sleepy, I'll not breathe a word. Ye see, that Joanna may be listenin', an' faith, if I don't believe she understands every word that's said about her!"

11 The Heroism
of Mr. Trouble

AT THE CORNER of Maple Avenue and Main Street,
where Padgett ruled from under his awninged stand, mysterious events were occurring. Sleepy wouldn't believe the
tale that Lover Carmichael reported to him, and so Lover
said, hurt and scornful, "Well, go see for yourself!"

"Now, Lover," Sleepy retorted indignantly, "you stop
pulling my leg! Once in a blue moon you might see a drunken
man in Northfield, but no one's ever seen a drunken *cat!*"

"You ask Padgett," squeaked Lover. "You ask anybody
on Main Street!"

Indeed, even though traffic came to a complete standstill,
Padgett willingly explained to everyone the new bedevil-
ment that had beset him.

"As I said before, and I'll say again, this town has become
shamefully demoralized," the policeman exhorted. "Not only
the people, mind you—now the corruption's spreading to the
cats."

"You mean," insisted Sleepy incredulously, "that you
actually caught a drunken cat?"

74

Padgett nodded soberly. He had been directing traffic, he said, when he saw the cat in the road. The animal approached him unsteadily. Its legs shivered and wobbled, as though the animal had been seized by an ague; and then its legs spread out in the road like the legs of an uncertain ice-skater and the cat skidded onto its belly. Once more the animal arose, still shivering and wobbling; and once more down it went, this time rolling over on its back and kicking its feet in the air. Cars honked on every side but now the cat refused to move.

"So I picked her up," continued the scandalized Padgett, "and 'twas then, young Mr. Jones, that I smelled her breath. I swear it was heavily scented with alcohol!"

Padgett looked angry when Sleepy still appeared dubious. But how could anyone believe a story like that?

Then from the firehouse emerged Rex, the fire company's dog. The canine came forward with slow, faltering steps; and stood by the curb, swaying. A fly, buzzing by Rex's nose, caused him to lift a paw in an effort to drive off the insect. Instead Rex toppled into the gutter with his face flattened out as though a fire engine had passed over it, and remained there with his rear portions elevated on slightly bowed legs. The dog's expression seemed sheepish and silly.

"The dogs are drunk, too!" Lover squeaked.

A red-faced Padgett promptly verified that fact. "'Tis the crazy house where I belong," the policeman growled. "There I'd be a happier man!"

Rex wagged his tail with an awkward, jerky motion. Someone called, "Up, Rex!" Always friendly, the dog tried to respond, but there were springs in the pads of Rex's paws that lifted him too high and thus landed him back in the gutter.

A voice shouted, "Throw him in jail, Padgett!"

"Where did he get it?"

"Yes, somebody's responsible for this!"

Against a nearby telephone pole Padgett's club beat a furious tattoo. Nothing would please him more, his belligerent manner said, than to lay his hands on the perpetrator of this deed!

Meanwhile Rex—the first dog ever to follow the example of a cat—rolled over on his back, clawed the air with all four paws, then lapsed into a blissful slumber. His tongue hung out the side of his mouth, increasing his appearance of silliness.

The crowd gathering at the corner of Maple Avenue and Main Street swelled rapidly. On the fringe of the group Sleepy noticed Kelly, and in the man's expression there was a suspiciously furtive quality. The boy crossed over to the Irishman.

"Kelly, do you know anything about this?"

"*Sssh*, me lad, or ye'll have me in the clink!"

"Kelly, what in thunder—"

"*Sssh!*" The Irishman forcefully drew Sleepy up the alley until they were by themselves behind the firehouse.

"Kelly, you ought to be ashamed—"

"Me!" blustered Kelly, regaining his composure. "'Tis not me so much as that Joanna who's at the bottom o' this! An', ye might say, the whole greedy nature o' the animal kingdom! Anyhow, I read that monkeys can't drink much whisky—it puts them right to sleep—so I hit upon the idea o' settin' out several saucers o' milk heavily spiked with likker, thinkin' that Joanna would find one. Well, mebbe she did an' turned up her nose at the concoction, an' then that cat an' dog—"

The peals of laughter that rolled out of Sleepy interrupted Kelly.

"Faith, an' *'tis* kind o' funny, ain't it?"

"Wait till they report this in the Culver City *Press!*"

Worry returned to cloud Kelly's eyes. "If the townspeople find out I'm behind this I'll be tarred an' feathered!"

"You sure will if Padgett has his way!"

Kelly's mouth tightened. "I'm not so scared o' him. One Irishman can handle another, me lad!"

"Boy, I'd like to see the two of you squared off!"

" 'Twould be an even fight," Kelly said with dignity. "An' a reasonably fair one. But if we keep our mouths shut, mebbe it can be avoided. Not that I won't tell Padgett in time, but 'tis better, don't ye think, to wait till the bloom o' his anger has faded?"

"But if he finds those saucers of milk and traces their origin—"

"He won't find them 'cause they won't be there to find!" Kelly, aware of the work involved in destroying this evidence, announced precipitately, "I'll be seein' ye, laddie. Now remember—mum's the word!"

A grinning Sleepy watched Kelly disappear around the firehouse. Actually the boy was under no obligation to report to Padgett what he knew. And deep in Sleepy's heart there was a tenderness for Kelly. The old Irishman would give any of them the shirt off his back.

Surprisingly, the afflicted cat and dog were not the main feature of the story that appeared that evening in the Culver City *Press*. True, they were mentioned, but the headlines still belonged to Joanna. For the next two weeks, the *Press* said, it would offer a reward of fifty dollars to anyone—or to any organized group of hunters—who succeeded in capturing the twelve-year-old Rhesus. The newspaper commented:

> It won't be easy. In fact, we doubt if it can be done. To us, it appears as though the community of Northfield has more than met its match in Joanna.
>
> And where do you think the monkey last was seen by our reporter? We'll tell you, for you'd never guess! She was perched on the front steps of the Northfield Public Library.
>
> Doubtless Joanna knows her own way in and out of the building and spent the evening reading. Perhaps she was studying up on bottle tricks and blanket tricks so that she would be prepared for the next ruse tried on her.
>
> Or perhaps she was checking on the gardening calendar. Early corn and tomatoes already have come into Northfield markets and soon will be ripe in Northfield gardens. Both these items are entirely acceptable in a monkey's diet, and Joanna is the kind of girl smart enough to look ahead!
>
> So we offer the reward of fifty dollars but we doubt if anyone will win it. About the only way Northfield ever will come to terms with Joanna is to make her mayor next election day!

Sleepy read down the column with his anger rising the further he progressed. This type of smart-aleck writing carried the joke too far!

"The *Press* is making Northfield look ridiculous," the boy complained to his father.

"Poking fun is all right, but only up to a limit," Mr. Jones agreed.

Mrs. Jones spoke heatedly. "If the *Press* really wants to report the facts, why don't they say most of the early corn coming into the market is wormy? I bought a dozen ears today and threw it all into the ash can!"

Sleepy sighed. With the Little League, the ball team, the Kylers, Joanna, Kelly, and the tipsy dog and cat, he guessed that he'd never forget this summer! And most people thought that Northfield was a quiet little hamlet where nothing ever happened!

The following morning events of a mysterious nature still were occurring in Northfield, but now their focal point had moved up Maple Avenue to the Jones residence. The six big packages that the man on the delivery truck deposited on the front porch brought Sleepy across the yard on the run.

"That's them, hey Mom?" he shouted. "That's the uniforms for the team?"

"It is," Mrs. Jones admitted. "And they can't be opened until Buzz and the other boys are here and they can be seen by the whole group at once. Now don't argue with me, Sleepy. It's your father's orders and it's the only fair way!"

Mr. Trouble seemed almost as excited as Sleepy. The three-year-old bounced up and down, shouting strenuously. "Uniform, uniform! Mr. Trouble want uniform!"

"Oh-oh," groaned Mrs. Jones. "Wait until Mr. Trouble finds out there's no uniform for him. Then we'll really have a conniption!"

Sleepy, however, felt that Mr. Trouble was his mother's worry. He dashed off to find Poke, Turkey, Lover, and the others. Behind him Mr. Trouble's chant rose to a shattering crescendo:

"Uniform, uniform! Mr. Trouble want uniform!"

Banned from the screened porch where the packages had been stored, Mr. Trouble sat on the front steps, brooding. In his three-year-old mind floated images: an old baseball cap of Sleepy's that rested in the garage, a sweater eight sizes too large that hung in the attic, an old scarf on a nail in the cellar that his mother threw around her shoulders when she ran out to snatch the clothes from the line before a sudden summer shower. Thus Mr. Trouble devised for himself a uniform, and the first item he set off to collect was Sleepy's forgotten baseball cap.

Around the side of the house marched Mr. Trouble, sucking his thumb. But his eyes, focusing on the rim of the trash can, beheld an object that darted in and out of sight.

Mr. Trouble stopped as though he had stepped into soft concrete and then had felt the mushy substance harden around his feet. The lid of the trash can lay upon the ground, and once more, as Mr. Trouble stared, the object—thin, furry, and bent on the end—flickered in and out of the boy's line of vision.

Mr. Trouble quietly moved forward and looked into the can. At almost the same moment Joanna, nibbling on the discarded ears of wormy corn, raised her head to look out.

So, nose to nose, they met. Whether Mr. Trouble or Joanna was the more startled was difficult to tell. Joanna ducked her head and Mr. Trouble ducked his. Both his eyes and hers were the size of saucers.

But Mr. Trouble, bending over, placed his hand directly on the cover of the trash can.

Joanna grew greedy. She paused for a few more nibbles. Over her head a dark cloud descended. Mr. Trouble had slammed the lid on the can!

The din of the ensuing moments became explosive. Joanna scrambled and screamed and tried to push off the lid. Mr. Trouble flung himself across the cover and bounded up and down each time Joanna thrashed against it. Meanwhile Mr. Trouble's lungs also exploded:

"Can, can! Monkey, monkey!"

Mr. Trouble's lungs possessed wonderful powers of penetration. He screeched "Ca-an-*nn!*" so that it sounded like an air raid siren. And his shrill "Mo-onk-kee-*eee!*" equaled

Nose to nose, they met.

in effect the blows of a sledgehammer against an empty boiler.

Joanna threw herself against the cover with a new burst of vigor at every shout.

But Mr. Trouble, spread belly-wise across the can, clung to his perilous perch, too frightened to let go.

From the back porch Mr. Trouble's mother came running. Up the driveway the mailman dashed with his delivery bag spanking him at every stride. Across the back yard sprinted Turkey Saunders's father still carrying three of the eggs he had been gathering in his hen-house.

"Mo-onk-kee-*eee!*" bellowed Mr. Trouble as mailman and bag, Mr. Saunders and eggs, and Mrs. Jones converged on the trash can.

Mrs. Jones snatched Mr. Trouble from his perch. Off flew the cover and up popped the head of a very angry Joanna.

Mr. Saunders, despite his considerable corpulence, now demonstrated that he was a man of action. Joanna's obvious intention was to scamper out of the can. But Mr. Saunders let sail an egg.

Joanna pulled back her head, startled. Streams of sticky, yellow yolk ran down her face.

And now the mailman recovered his wits. Down on top of the trash can went his heavy bag with Joanna still trapped inside.

"Egg, egg!" screamed Mr. Trouble, delighted.

Mr. Saunders laughed. "It's my old pitching arm that Turkey's inherited," he boasted. "But Mr. Trouble's the real hero. With this whole town chasing that monkey it took a three-year-old to capture her and win the reward of fifty dollars!"

The heroism of Mr. Trouble, said Sleepy's father at the

unveiling of the uniforms that afternoon, was more important than any of them suspected.

"For," he continued, "when we bought these uniforms we expected Joanna to be caught, and when she wasn't it looked as though *our* joke had backfired."

Mr. Jones held up a uniform. Across the chest in big black letters was the word Northfield, and directly underneath was the figure of a miniature Joanna!

"Well," Mr. Jones explained, "our idea was to say to the rest of the county: 'Northfield can handle Joanna—but can you?'"

The grin that spread across Sleepy's face was on Poke's face, and Lover's, and on Hutch Bannister's. Someone giggled. Then laughter broke out on all sides.

"That's what we'll do," Tennessee Martin proclaimed. "It's our turn now to make monkeys out of *them!*"

12 A Team
in the Making

FOR PADGETT, the capture of Joanna restored peace and dignity to Northfield. Once more, whistle in mouth, the policeman ruled from his awninged stand at Maple and Main, concentrating his attention on ferreting out potential traffic violators. Once more Padgett remained alert to jaywalkers, hustling them back onto the sidewalk with bristling warnings that their continued carelessness would lead them into court, for in Padgett's experience a thoughtless pedestrian was as dangerous as the impatient motorist who raced his engine and started his automobile moving before the traffic light had switched from amber to green.

For Sleepy, however, Joanna's return to her chain under the arbor of the Kyler home on Locust Street far from deprived the summer of its mounting excitement. Insofar as all the merchants of Northfield had contributed to the purchase of the uniforms, a walk along Main Street stimulated a barrage of comments: "How's that team coming, Sleepy?" "We're counting on you boys to come through with a winner!" If there were fewer mosquitoes in Northfield than in previous summers, Sleepy didn't wonder. There was too much baseball in the air to leave room for mere insects!

On the following Monday when Sleepy set off for practice only one thought filled his mind. Just one week separated Northfield from its opening game against Culver City! Unless Sleepy missed his guess, this would be a week when Buzz would crack down. Seven days—six only, since Sunday was a day of worship in Northfield—to whip into shape the team that would have the impudence to flaunt the symbol of Joanna's sassiness! Kelly, who refused to be left out of the fun, declared that he would bring Joanna to the games as the team's mascot.

"Faith, an' there she'll be as large as life sittin' besides me on the bench," the Irishman boasted.

Faith, thought Sleepy, unless Northfield played fast, hardheaded baseball, Joanna was a joke that sure could backfire!

Deep in these meditations, Sleepy approached the ball field without noticing the stranger waiting there. The man, Sleepy judged, was about Buzz's age. Dressed in a checked suit, the newcomer wore a fedora hat pushed back on his broad, sloping forehead. Sleepy was seized with the ridiculous notion that if the stranger had been cloaked in a tunic and feathered headdress and had carried a tomahawk he would have made a perfect model for an old-time cigar store Indian.

"I'm Dixie Bell," the man said. "If you haven't heard of me, you will. I'm sports editor of the Culver City *Press*."

Sleepy nodded uneasily. In Dixie Bell's voice was that note of petulant importance that sometimes crept into Turkey's voice and made Turkey so difficult to live with. Moreover Sleepy wondered why Dixie singled him out. True, it was still early for practice with only four or five other boys in the field shagging the flies that Poke hit, but why hadn't Dixie announced his presence to them? The sports editor supplied an answer.

"That fat kid over there—his name is Poke, I think—told me you were responsible for getting Buzz to coach the Northfield team."

Sleepy said, "My dad did that."

Dixie mopped his forehead, for the sun seemed to find that broad expanse of reddened skin to its special liking. "Will Buzz be here soon?"

"Any minute now."

"Well, it's a good story," Dixie said. "I saw Buzz play that last season in the minors—saw him, in fact, on the night when he slammed down his glove in the locker room and declared that he was through with baseball forever. Now you kids have brought him back to the game. That's quite a yarn!"

Sleepy still didn't like Dixie's tone; the sports editor appeared to be prodding, as though, as Lover would say, he smelled a den in Ratmark. Fortunately the others on the team soon arrived, Buzz among them. The former Yankee star greeted the sports writer in a pleasant manner and answered his questions easily. Buzz admitted quite cheerfully that his return to baseball had surprised him as much as anyone and said that part of the responsibility for his change of heart belonged to Joanna.

"In what way?" Dixie asked.

"In leading me to this nice group of kids," Buzz answered.

Sleepy guessed that he had been all wrong in his hunch about Dixie. But then, Sleepy learned almost at once, he had been wrong on another count.

"Why sure," Buzz said in response to one of Dixie's

queries, "I can give you our probable starting line-up for the Culver City game. Turkey Saunders will pitch and Poke Johnson will catch. At first we'll play Sleepy Jones and at second I'm starting Lover Carmichael. At short—"

Sleepy stopped eavesdropping. Lover at second! Was Buzz touched in the head? Lover couldn't play the infield! It was all right to admire Lover's willingness to keep plugging, but what was going to happen to the center of the infield's defense if a flub-dub like Hutch Bannister at short was paired off with a bigger flub-dub like Lover at second?

When practice started Dixie had left, and Buzz, placing Lover on second, appeared to feel that this decision was reasonable. The light of the reborn Lover shone in the new infielder's eyes as it had that first day under Buzz when Lover finally had beaten out a bunt.

Buzz's coaching was persistent and patient:

"Look, Lover, with these shorter base paths in Little League baseball, you've got to hold the runner close to the bag. You stay right there on the base, not giving the runner an inch of lead, until Turkey takes his turn to pitch to the plate. Then you scoot back to your normal fielding position to cover a ball hit that way. You've got to keep digging all the time. There's nothing a second baseman needs like a sturdy pair of legs."

Lover nodded intensely. One thing you could say for Buzz, he made you see why baseball was played the way it was. And logic gave the game more meaning. Even Sleepy, watching Lover bob back and forth, first toward the bag and then to his fielding depth, understood Lover's stamina for playing second. Maybe Buzz was right. With Lover on second, Tennessee Martin was freed to play center field. Tennessee's loping gait was better than Lover's for patrolling these outer reaches, Tennessee's stronger throwing arm better for whipping a hit back into the infield.

Buzz made the rounds from position to position, pounding principles home.

"You, Poke!" he roared. "Get that mask off quicker on a pop foul. Time saved means distance. One foot, two feet can make the difference between a foul strike and a foul out. Baseball is movement. Keep on the go. All the time."

Poke tested the fit of his mask after that each time he crouched behind the plate. Buzz smiled.

Principles. Tricks that made a ball player better than average. Buzz wouldn't let up. A good fielder used both hands on a catch, cradling the ball in his glove and clamping down with his "meat" hand to make sure it didn't pop out. A shortstop took the ball in front of him without breaking his stride, coming on it with body low and knees bent so that he could jump up quickly if the ball took an unexpected hop. A runner leading down off base kept his weight on the balls of his feet, his arms loose and moving easily back and forth so that he was charged up at any instant to break and run.

Maybe a fellow couldn't remember all the lore of baseball that poured out of Buzz, Sleepy thought, but a large part of it was certain to stick. Then Buzz stood behind Sleepy, driving home the technique of playing first base.

"Keep those wrists flexible, Sleepy. You've got to be able to take a hit or a throw from almost any angle. You've got to obtain all the stretch you can, so just let your toe touch the bag on a throw. You take the grounders to your right that are hard hit, but if they're slow rollers let Lover handle them while you hustle over to cover the sack!"

Timing and judgment, Buzz preached. Sheer ability wasn't enough. You needed to think. Men like Marty Marion and Phil Rizzuto and Stan Musial were baseball headliners because they backed up brawn with brain.

Later when Sleepy was stretched out on the grass waiting his turn at bat, Tennessee dropped down beside him.

"Buzz is making a team out of us," Tennessee said.

Sleepy watched Lover digging after a grounder. Knees bent, Lover grabbed the ball and flipped underhand to Asphalt, who now covered first. Even Lover was learning.

"That high squeak of Lover's," Tennessee grinned. "You hear it all the time—even in the outfield."

Sleepy nodded. Lover could be a spark—something every team could use—if he could only come through under pressure. Practice was one thing; you had the chance then to keep trying a play till you got it right. But in a game you had only one chance. There would be the big gamble with Lover, and Sleepy hoped that Buzz would be proved right.

And right with Turkey, too. Buzz still insisted that Turkey take a dozen swings a day at that mark on the tree trunk. But anyone could sense Turkey's inward rebellion, the half-hearted effort he put into this performance. Funny how two guys could be so stubborn—Turkey and Buzz. And where hitting was concerned, Turkey showed scant improvement.

"It's a lost cause," Sleepy averred.

When Tennessee rolled over in the grass, his long, angular body seemed to uncoil like a serpent. Tennessee was a grass chewer like Lover, and in moments of leisure he liked to root around in the grass looking for four-leaf clovers. His record discovery for one summer was forty-two, but this year he aspired to finding an even fifty.

"Turkey's a darn fool," he opined now in answer to Sleepy's comment. "If he'd only try he'd end the agony."

"We need Turkey!"

"Not as much as we need Buzz," Tennessee replied laconically, but when Sleepy looked up, hoping to judge precisely what Tennessee did mean, the other boy was occupied prodding the grass in quest of his new record.

In the end, Sleepy decided that he worried too much— about Turkey, about Lover and Hutch, about everything. Certainly when Dixie Bell's story appeared in the Culver City *Press,* no team could have asked for friendlier publicity. Every line Dixie wrote about Buzz and the boys had a warm ring. Dixie said:

> With Buzz Kyler behind them, this Northfield team can be the dark horse surprising the favorites in the Little League. Like Joanna, once these Northfield diamond dusters shake loose, they may be very hard to catch.

"Now that's fine," Mr. Jones said. "Buzz has done a good job and this opening game at Culver City should draw quite a crowd. Your mother and I are driving down with Mr. Trouble."

Well, that would or wouldn't be fine, Sleepy decided, depending on how the team made out. The attraction of the approaching game increased as the days passed, and the merchants of Northfield voted at their Thursday Luncheon Club meeting to hire a bus to transport the team to Culver City. But the most spectacular announcement came from Kelly.

"Ye know," he told Sleepy, "I'm escortin' Joanna to the game."

"You'll need help."

"I've got it, me lad. Padgett's ridin' down with me!"

"You mean Padgett's going to be seen in public with a monkey?"

"An' who are ye referrin' to, me or Joanna?" Kelly asked with feigned irritability. "Seriously now, there's a mite o' satisfaction to Padgett in havin' that Rhesus in captivity."

"Wait till he finds out what *you* did to that cat and dog!"

" 'Twas a well intentioned deed," Kelly said with dignity, "as I've already explained to him. I'm not denyin' that the first few moments o' me confession weren't difficult—if there had been a pair o' shillelaghs around we doubtless would have killed each other—but then we saw that what was done couldn't be undone, an' so we shook hands for underneath the Irish are a forgivin' people."

An impish thought struck Sleepy. "How does Joanna feel about all this?"

Kelly sighed. "Now there," he said, "ye have me. 'Twill be a situation that will put Padgett on his mettle."

That, reflected Sleepy with a grin, was stating the case mildly. "Will Johnny ride down with you?"

"No," Kelly replied offhandedly. "He's goin' down on the bus."

"But he hasn't even been out for practice!"

Kelly's Irish guile never had seemed more calculating.

" 'Tis true. But then he won't be in uniform, so no harm should come o' it." Kelly's voice dropped almost to a whisper. "See here, Sleepy me boy, I've had this out with Buzz an' I don't want any trouble with you!"

Sometimes, Sleepy thought, the Irishman's secretive manner could be infuriating. "You're not telling me everything!"

"So I'm not," Kelly responded airily. " 'Tis a very annoyin' habit I've cultivated o' late!"

And so saying, Kelly turned on his heels and walked away.

13 Bases
Loaded

ON THE BUS trip to Culver City, Johnny rode beside
Sleepy. Alone of the boys in the vehicle, Johnny wore dungarees and a sports shirt and his garb looked painfully conspicuous surrounded by all the new Northfield uniforms.
Johnny was a misfit, Sleepy decided sadly. It was too bad.

"Every night Kelly and I practice," Johnny muttered, as
though trying to atone for the awkwardness of his position.

But Sleepy's thoughts had skipped elsewhere. He wondered how Kelly and Padgett were faring as Joanna's escort.
A grin stole across his lips at the complications that could
beset that journey. Then, conscious of the embarrassed silence that had grown between Johnny and himself, he asked:
"How's Kelly as a coach?"

"Ye can have worse," Johnny retorted, imitating the Irishman's tone as well as his language. "He's a stubborn man,
that Kelly. And he has ideas."

"Sometimes they work and sometimes they don't," said
Sleepy, remembering Rex sprawled on the pavement in front

of the fire house. "So Kelly's determined that you'll be an infielder?"

"No—not since the night I got mad." Johnny had been
around Kelly so long that he had absorbed the Irishman's
gift for giving even a simple story an atmosphere of deep
mystery. "One night a grounder that Kelly threw hit a
stump and bounced off my noggin. I picked up the ball, sore
as a wet hen, and slammed it back at Kelly. 'Can ye do that
again?' Kelly asked. I heaved another hard one at him. 'Now,
with just a twist o' yer wrist,' he said. So I pegged one, giving my wrist a turn as I let go of the ball. And now, if you
can believe Kelly, I'm a pitcher!"

"What do you believe?"

"I think I am, too."

Sleepy turned around, surprised. Johnny had spoken with
quiet confidence. At that moment the bus ground noisily up
a hill, and Johnny's eyes, while watching the passing countryside, seemed focused on some point that no one but he
could see. He said, "Who knows? A pitcher would be something new in the Kyler family!"

Another good pitcher would be something that the Northfield team could darn well use, Sleepy might have answered.
The thought of Asphalt Smith as the only relief hurler they
had when Turkey's arm tightened was not altogether comforting. If Johnny could develop—

"Time will tell," the other boy said. "Time—and Kelly's
patience."

Sleepy nodded. Meanwhile other matters pressed upon his
mind. In another hour they would have completed their
warm-up practice at the Culver City ball field, and the umpire would be striding out to the plate to call, "Play ball!"

In the six fast-paced innings of the Little League game that would follow, much would depend on Turkey. If only the old Turk would keep his control—if only that Adam's apple didn't begin bobbing up and down—they'd have a chance!

Sleepy's glance stole along the aisle of the bus and rested on Turkey. The pitcher appeared relaxed, but at least part of the credit for that fact belonged to Lover, an inveterate clown, who was mimicking Padgett directing traffic.

"Lover's good for a team," Johnny said. "He's a kind of pop-off guy for everybody's taut nerves."

Sleepy sighed. Lover was a spark all right—a spark that they badly needed—and yet here was another great riddle that the coming afternoon must reveal. Under pressure, could Lover make the mark? As if to answer Sleepy's question, Lover's squeaky voice boomed forth in a recitation:

> *There was ease in Casey's manner as he*
> *   stepped into his place,*
> *There was pride in Casey's bearing, and*
> *   a smile lit Casey's face,*
> *And when, responding to the cheers, he*
> *   lightly doffed his hat,*
> *No stranger in the crowd could doubt*
> *   'twas Casey at the bat.*

The lines of *Casey At The Bat* rolled on until Lover reached the point where Mudville's mighty slugger swung and miffed; then, with a roar, the whole team chorused:

> *"Strike one," the umpire said.*

Buzz laughed with the others and his eyes, resting on Lover, appeared gentle. Buzz had been shrewd in understanding what Lover could mean to a team. What was more, Sleepy asked himself, why was he so het up over Turkey or Lover? His big problem was whether, under real game conditions, Sleepy Jones, Esquire, could come through as Northfield's first baseman!

In a sudden panic, Sleepy tried to remember all the tricks Buzz had taught him about handling his position. Play the ball rather than the base; go after that ball, Buzz had preached, and rely on your speed to carry you back to the base ahead of the runner. Each rule Buzz had prescribed came back to Sleepy as the bus sped on. The outskirts of Culver City flashed by, then the bus weaved and honked through the main arteries of the downtown business section. A few moments later the vehicle swung into a park, and there before them stretched the benches, the diamond, the crowd gathering to watch the game!

Kelly and Padgett, with Joanna in tow, were among the first to greet the boys when they tumbled out of the bus.

" 'Tis a great day for the Irish," Kelly boasted. His arm was linked through Padgett's.

Joanna strained against her chain, chattering excitedly.

Sleepy's glance searched through the crowd till it found Mr. Trouble and his parents. The grownups waved, but Mr. Trouble took no heed of anything except his ice cream cone. When Sleepy turned back he noticed that Johnny had moved off with Kelly and Padgett. The Culver City fans gathered around Joanna, who stared back with the haughty disdain that she reserved for the human race.

Muscles tightened in Sleepy's stomach when he dashed onto the field for the pre-game warm-up, but after he had scooped a grounder from the dirt and whipped the ball across the infield to Asphalt at third Sleepy's tenseness began to ease. Soon he was gaping at the Culver City players, sizing them up critically, and thinking, "Huh, they don't look so tough!"

But the Culver City nine proved to be much tougher than Sleepy suspected. The opposing pitcher, a tall, spindle-legged boy with the melodious name of McGillicuddy, demonstrated his prowess when Northfield came to bat in the top of the first inning. McGillicuddy possessed speed and a tricky curve that bit the corners of the plate. Asphalt struck out, Tennessee might as well have stopped to search for four-leaf clovers for all the chance he had of beating out a weak roller to the mound, and Hutch popped up to the catcher.

The Culver City stands hooted derisively, "Cage those monkeys! Put 'em all on chains!"

Sleepy supposed that with Joanna for a mascot they had to expect this sort of ribbing. Still, a joke could be carried too far!

The Culver City rooters were ready to carry the joke just as far as they could—twice around the world, if possible. When the first Culver City batter smashed a single over third, a chant went up:

"Those guys belong back in the trees—not on a ball field!"

Holding the bag against the runner, Sleepy wiped the sweat from his face and managed a grin. Underneath, however, the tenseness crept back into Sleepy's stomach. Turkey's control wobbled. The next Culver City batsman walked on four straight pitches.

"Never mind," Lover squeaked gamely. "We'll get the next one!"

But the boiled-beet look had returned to little Lover's face. He, too, was on edge—like Turkey, whose Adam's apple bobbed once; like Hutch at short, who nervously pounded his fist into his glove.

And again the Culver City crowd cried scornfully: "You got 'em up a tree! That pitcher belongs in the Ape League! Teach 'em some real monkey shines!"

On the bench Buzz Kyler smiled quietly. Sleepy took a hitch in his belt and thought: "Poor Buzz, he's coming back to baseball just the way he left it—with the fans down his neck!" The first baseman was almost afraid to glance at Johnny, huddled on the bench between Kelly and Padgett. Did Johnny look so small because that was the way he felt?

Turkey threw a ball, then a strike, but his control remained shaky. The count went to three-and-two and then Poke had to dive to smother a low curve that was a foot wide. The batter, grinning, tossed aside his club and trotted down to first. Bases loaded—and no outs!

"We'll score a million runs!" screamed one Culver City partisan.

The palm of Sleepy's glove hand felt wet. The Culver City clean-up hitter came to the plate with a free-moving, confident stride. Turkey swallowed miserably. His pitch sailed in, the bat connected, and the ball streaked across the infield.

"Into the hole at second!" yipped the noisy Culver City partisan. "It'll be good for a double! It'll clean the bases! It'll—"

Little Lover dove. Head, back, legs—Lover turned over completely. He was sprawled flat on the ground when Sleepy saw the ball again—in Lover's hand!

Hutch, racing for second, took Lover's throw. Little Lover,

still sitting, grinned broadly as Hutch touched the bag ahead of the runner.

Then Hutch turned. The long throw from second to home seemed hopeless with the runner from third scampering wildly down the base path. But across the plate stood Poke, mitt raised, legs spread against the impact of the slide. Hutch threw with all the strength he possessed.

The umpire stood over the plate as the sliding runner, the ball, and Poke's big mitt all struck at once. A cloud of dust swirled upward. And the umpire, hand swinging over his shoulder, sang, *"You're out!"*

Little Lover and Hutch—and what a play! Sleepy didn't care if tears were rolling down his cheeks. This was base-ball—team baseball—baseball that might be too big for a fellow's head, but not for his heart!

On the Northfield bench Buzz Kyler still smiled quietly. Perhaps it was the proud, cocky lift of Lover's head that Buzz noticed.

Culver City continued to threaten, with a runner on first and second, but Sleepy felt now that the home team wouldn't score. A towering fly was the best the next batter could achieve. Sleepy made the catch near the stands, and a disappointed rival fan growled, "Lucky!"

Sleepy tipped his cap to his critic. "You mean agile," he flung back. "Like a monkey!"

Buzz's voice was gentle.

"Boys, I don't care what the final score is. We've won the big thing—the drive to keep plugging even when the cause seems lost! You're going to win a lot of ball games!"

Sleepy felt that Northfield would win this game right there and then, but he was wrong. McGillicuddy, the spindly

Culver City pitcher, also possessed a fighting heart. Again he blanked his opposition, and, growing stronger as the game neared its scheduled length of six innings, he added zeros to the Northfield score in the third, fourth, and fifth.

"He's tough," Sleepy admitted, going down on strikes for the second time. In fact, only a scratch single by the be-spectacled Shad Rowe marred McGillicuddy's performance.

"We're tough too," Lover boasted.

Four scattered hits were all Turkey had yielded after righting himself from that almost fatal first inning. Now Turkey pitched through the fifth without giving up a run.

Lover, first up in the sixth, stopped to whisper with Buzz. Then, on McGillicuddy's first pitch, Lover bunted. Ball, bat, and Lover all started moving at once. Lover knew how to take his coaching.

Lover beat the throw to first by a step. The Northfield stands rose with a cheer and when Kelly jumped up Joanna, stimulated by the quickening excitement, raced around in leaping circles.

"If we can just get one run," Sleepy prayed, as Poke, swinging his bat, strode to the plate. Buzz would want Poke to sacrifice Lover to second, in scoring position, where Shad Rowe could drive him home with a single.

Poke bunted. Lover, off with the forward motion of the pitcher's arm, raced into second, standing up. The only play Culver City could make was to nip Poke at first.

Shad faced McGillicuddy, squinting fiercely through his glasses. The Culver City hurler went back to the rosin bag, wanting to take the time to think through how he would pitch to Shad. There was a coolness to this spindle-legged lad that you had to admire, Sleepy admitted. Thus far McGillicuddy had handcuffed Northfield most effectively, and before the Little League season ended he likely would do so again—perhaps more than once.

The first pitch was a fast ball, right across the letters of Shad's uniform, that went for a called strike. Shad backed out of the batter's box, dusted his hands, and stepped to the plate once more, tight-lipped and determined.

A gnawing uneasiness crept over Sleepy. If Shad failed to hit, Turkey would be next up. What chance would he have of bringing home Lover? Turkey hadn't even tried to take his coaching, and the chance of victory that Lover had earned them because the second baseman had buckled down would be ruined! Buzz would have to string along with Turkey; Asphalt couldn't be trusted to relieve in a game as close as this.

"It's Shad or nothing," growled Sleepy, sick to think how Turkey's stubbornness now could spoil everything.

At the sound of Shad's bat meeting the ball, the whole bench leaped up. Then sickness settled heavily in every Northfield stomach. Shad had topped one of McGillicuddy's screwballs, and though Lover raced on to third, Shad was an easy out at first.

McGillicuddy broke into a smile. There was only Turkey to retire; the inning was as good as over. Turkey went down on three straight pitches.

Sleepy tried not to meet Turkey's glance or reveal his intense disappointment and resentment. Lover chirped cheerfully, "We'll get 'em next time up," but against a hurler of McGillicuddy's power, how many chances to score might there be? Turkey couldn't help but sense the brittleness all around him.

Culver City struck suddenly—two sharp, stinging doubles —and a run was in and the game ended. The home stands screamed gleefully.

Sleepy, stuffing his mitt in his hip pocket, wondered what Buzz thought. But the coach did not indulge in recriminations.

"We'll get another chance at these guys," Buzz said.

Asphalt, swinging along beside Sleepy, spoke more bitterly. "Next time Turkey swings at that tree in practice he better start hitting the mark!"

Shad wanted to take all the blame. "If I had connected, it'd been a different story!"

But Asphalt simply snorted. "You tried—you gave us a chance—and topping that screwball was just one of the breaks of baseball. Turkey didn't even give us a chance!"

On the ride back on the bus, Lover and Buzz alone acted cheerful. Turkey sat quietly—thinking through, Sleepy hoped, how right Buzz had been in trying to teach him the rudiments of hitting.

"I feel sorry for that guy," Johnny Kyler murmured.

Sleepy stirred rebelliously. "Why?"

"Everybody flops—now and then."

"It was Turkey's own fault."

"Maybe," Johnny said. "Anyhow, it can't be undone now. And there will be other games."

Sleepy nodded. If Turkey had learned from the experience, fine! Maybe he'd get it through his head at last that a team belonged to *nine* fellows. In the sudden silence that settled over the bus, the irrepressible Lover boomed forth:

> *Oh, somewhere in this favored land the*
> *sun is shining bright:*

The band is playing somewhere, and
somewhere hearts are light;
And somewhere men are laughing and little
children shout,
But there is no joy in Mudville, great
Casey has struck out.

Buzz laughed. "Lover," he said, "you've got the spirit of a champion—hanged if you haven't!"

14 At
Echo Lake

THE PICNIC to Echo Lake was Buzz's idea. Too much baseball, Buzz said, would wear down a fellow just as surely as too much cake or too much sun-bathing. What the team needed most, the coach declared, was to have fun and to forget the Culver City game now behind them or the contest with Franklinville that would be next on the schedule.

So the boys that gathered at the meadow, expecting a stiff, blistering session to iron out the weaknesses revealed by the defeat at Culver City, drove away instead in three cars for Echo Lake. Sleepy rode with Lover, Johnny, Hutch, and Dodo Newson in Kelly's old Ford.

"I put it up to you, Sleepy," said Dodo from behind the familiar squint of his sober countenance. "Do you know what to expect next?"

"Nobody knows from nothin' any more," Sleepy confessed.

Lover laughed. "Life hasn't been the same since Joanna popped into town! Anyhow, an outing to Echo Lake will be swell."

No one disputed Lover's statement. Echo Lake's bathing pavilion, boat houses, ball fields, Ferris Wheel, golf driving range, and other amusements made it a favorite vacation retreat.

"I heard," Hutch volunteered, "that they've got one of those new batting ranges where a machine slings the ball at you as fast as a big league pitcher."

"That'll be a good place for Turkey," Dodo grumbled. "We'll see that he spends all afternoon there."

Kelly coughed reprovingly. "Ye've had yer orders. Baseball is to be kept to a minimum today. So, Dodo, hold yer tongue about the old Turk!"

Holding your tongue still didn't stop you from thinking, Sleepy reflected. The resentment was pretty widespread over the fact that the Culver City game might never have been lost if Turkey had given them a fair chance at bat. And Dodo had a right to squawk. He had played a steady game in left field, handling without an error the three flies that had been hit his way.

In the strained silence of the moment, Johnny said, "Dad called Sleepy's father and asked him to pass on the news about the picnic. The upshot is that several dads have decided to come up after work to join us at Echo Lake. They're bringing up hot dogs and steaks for supper."

"Ah," quoted Lover glibly, " 'the fool that eats till he is sick must fast till he is well.' "

"Faith," averred Kelly, "this boy is a book with pants on!"

Hutch giggled. "He can recite 'em but he can't spell 'em!"

"Couldn't," corrected Lover. "But I've been plugging away every morning, and I'm getting pretty good. Also I found me the longest word in the dictionary and I can spell that. Listen: a-n-t-i-d-i-s-e-s-t-a-b-l-i-s-h-m-e-n-t-a-r-i-a-n-i-s-m!"

"What does it mean?" Hutch demanded.

"It means," replied Lover unflinchingly, "that your sister's in love with a hod carrier and they've run away to South America to start a revolution. Any more questions?"

"Thank you," said Hutch with dignity. "It is always a pleasure to know that you can recognize a liar when you meet one."

"That's exactly what your sister said to the hod carrier," continued an unabashed Lover, while the others chuckled. "It was too hot in South America to start a revolution, so they moved to Bouganville. Now in Bouganville—"

"Where's Bouganville?" Hutch insisted.

"Next to Louisville, you sap. In one town they make Louisville Sluggers and in the other they make the bats with holes in 'em that you use. Now in Bouganville—"

What really happened in the mythical city of Bouganville was that Hutch tossed Kelly's car blanket over Lover's head and held it there until Lover promised to remain quiet until they had reached Echo Lake.

Sleepy thought, a bit enviously, that of all the members of the team, the summer was turning out best for Lover. From a kid who only a month ago had been scared of mere shadows, Lover had developed into a self-confident guy who belonged with the crowd. Everything had become fun for Lover—even spelling.

When Sleepy tried to reckon what thus far the summer had meant to him he didn't seem to come off quite so well. He wished that he knew why, too. He got along all right—with the fellows and on the team—but still in unguarded moments he was seized by an uneasy feeling.

Why didn't he come right out and admit the truth? There had been that incident at breakfast when his dad had seemed to lose his appetite.

"I guess I'm wearing out," Mr. Jones had said, attempting to laugh off his sluggishness.

"You mean," Sleepy's mother had replied, "that you're working too hard!"

Neither parent had said anything to Sleepy, but he had stirred uncomfortably. Perhaps if he had helped out at the store—

Gosh, Sleepy thought now, couldn't a fellow work himself up into a real stew when he let his imagination become overactive? Wasn't his dad coming up that evening to join the picnic? Nothing very serious could be wrong if he could make that quick a recovery!

Kelly's old Ford chugged up a hill, and Sleepy, feeling better, listened to Johnny, Hutch, and Dodo harmonizing to *Sweet Adeline.* Lover's voice was no good for singing, unless his squeak could be used to imitate the train whistle in *Casey Jones.* Kelly smiled, and hummed along off key, and when it seemed appropriate beeped the horn for sound effects. The other cars had passed the ancient Ford long ago, but, Sleepy decided, it could only be a couple of miles further to Echo Lake, and as though to confirm this guess a big marker appeared on the road side.

"A twist an' a turn an' ye'll be there," Kelly announced. He proved to be not very far wrong.

Buzz paid for the rides on the Ferris Wheel and the scenic railroad. Lover, declaring that he must live up to his nickname, rode along through the Tunnel of Love and emerged from those dark passages swearing that he had seen a corpse in the water.

"I recognized the body," Lover testified solemnly. "It was McGillicuddy, the Culver City pitcher. His arm went lame and he committed suicide!"

This time the curve broke more sharply.

"But that he would," sighed Tennessee, remembering his own futile performance against that spindle-legged hurler.

A picnicking grove separated the amusement area from the bathing pavilion and the boat houses. When Lover organized a rescue party to follow him back into the Tunnel of Love after the fictitious corpse of McGillicuddy, a disinterested Sleepy wandered down into the grove. There he found Kelly crouched low behind a catcher's mitt while Johnny pivoted and whipped the ball across the piece of flagstone they used for a plate.

In the short time Johnny had practiced he couldn't have acquired all that pitching style, Sleepy told himself. Johnny's easy swing, the way his leg came up to give him greater power, must be natural to him. Sleepy admired the way that only Johnny's body faced the catcher until he threw, so that the ball shot out unexpectedly. That position would be nettlesome both to batters and base runners, for until the last moment no one could tell whether Johnny intended to throw to the plate or the bag.

At times, Sleepy thought, Johnny's fast ball stayed too high, as though it floated instead of spanking down toward the plate, and when Kelly called for a curve the pitch seemed away wide.

"Ye don't get a Bob Feller overnight," the Irishman commented, undisturbed. "Anyhow, some umps would be so blind they'd think that throw was a strike!"

"It's breaking too slow," Johnny complained.

"Then snap yer wrist harder."

This time the curve broke more sharply. Johnny's speed was impressive.

"What do ye think?" Kelly asked Sleepy.

"He could be hard to hit if his control holds up."

"Verra hard, me lad. Right now he'd walk eight out o' nine batters, but 'tis only confidence he needs, an' confidence is like a fickle woman for it takes a bit o' coaxin'.'"

"I like to throw low stuff," Johnny said, "but it's tough to handle."

"Poke will handle it," Sleepy answered.

"I hope so. Still, I dunno. A sinker's fine if it stays out of the dirt. But it can bounce and knock your head loose."

"An' without beggin' yer pardon," appended Kelly.

It seemed to Sleepy as though Johnny's pitching had come a long way. A hope glimmered brightly. If Johnny had been able to step in to relieve in the Culver City game so that Buzz could have sent in a pinch hitter for Turkey—well, who knew?

Turning, Sleepy saw Turkey. The scrawny boy also was watching Johnny—watching while he sucked on his lower lip.

"Doggone," Sleepy muttered, "that's a possibility, too. Johnny could make a starting pitcher!"

Well, let Turkey watch and take heed. Maybe next time Buzz asked Turkey to swing at that mark on the tree the old Turk would put some heart into the effort!

Kelly and Johnny had quit their practice when the others came down from the Tunnel of Love. This time, Tennessee declared, there *had* been a corpse in the water, although not the corpse of McGillicuddy.

"You know how it is in those places," Tennessee said. "All dark and spooky. You drift along until you come to a lighted space where they have waxed figures in various scenes. In one Indians were scalping little children and in another a poor old mother was sobbing her heart out as they hoisted her son to the gallows. I don't know what all that violence has to do with lovemaking, but then I've never been in love.

"Anyhow, Lover's drifting along in the boat, trailing his hand in the water and telling us we ain't seen nothin' till we get to the scene of everybody dying during a cholera plague. It's sure creepy in there. Dodo's hanging onto Shad and Poke's throat is gurgling like a bullfrog's.

"Then Lover's hand touches something. He doesn't bother to reason it's one of the waxed figures that's fallen into the water. He just lets out a yell that would curdle your blood. Shad wants to jump out of the boat and Hutch swears he can see someone with a bloody knife crouching against the wall. It's so dark now you can't see the tip of your nose, but Hutch has got x-ray eyes and recognizes that bloody knife. Boy, what a mess!"

Lover grinned sheepishly. "If I fall over in a faint," he said, "will somebody rush back into that tunnel and get my heart? I think it popped out of my mouth when I yelled."

Dodo cackled. "Tennessee wasn't any hero. We drifted around the next turn and there was that cholera plague. Rats gnawing at the stiffs and all that pleasant stuff. Tennessee's eyes would have bulged right out of their sockets if I hadn't shoved 'em back!"

Buzz shook his head. The purpose of the picnic at Echo Lake had been to give the team a rest. Still, no one could deny that the Tunnel of Love had diverted their minds from baseball.

"The terror of McGillicuddy will be nothing after that," Shad pronounced.

Hunger had begun to nibble at the fringes of Sleepy's stomach when the older men arrived to join the boys. Soon a crackling fire blazed in the grove and steaks dripped succulently on the turning spits. Turkey Saunders's dad played a harmonica, and Dodo Newson's father, almost as sober-faced as his son, danced a jig. Sleepy guessed that he never had known a better time, and Asphalt Smith, eating almost constantly, paused long enough to sing out:

"What's the matter with Buzz K?"

A chorus responded lustily:

"He's all right!"

Sleepy glanced at Johnny's countenance alight with pleasure. Tonight was some different, Sleepy wagered, from that night in the minor league when Buzz had been booed off the field!

Afterward there were games and the boys opposed their fathers in a sack race. The older men did well, but the boys had the advantage—by virtue of the fact, Turkey Saunders's dad declared, that they had more ants in their pants. Then Sleepy saw his father standing by the fire, holding his side.

"It's nothing—just a muscle kink," Mr. Jones told Buzz.

"Still, you better take it easy," Buzz cautioned.

Mr. Jones stood erect. "There, it's better. I'm just imagining things, I guess."

Sleepy looked away, troubled. Twice in one day his dad had acted in this queer manner!

15 Who's a Monkey Now?

THE FRANKLINVILLE game, the first to be played on Northfield's home grounds, produced almost as many unexpected incidents as the picnic to Echo Lake. Padgett's offer to umpire met with general approval, since Padgett was a judicious and fair-minded man, but there was one dissenting voice.

The objector was Joanna. Ever since the day when the monkey had climbed on top of the awninged traffic stand and Padgett had come after her with his nightstick between his teeth, the animosity between these two had been deep-seated. Now the sight of Padgett in an umpire's mask and chest protector aroused violent emotions in Joanna.

Whenever Padgett called out "Str-*rike!*" Joanna strained on her chain and bared her teeth at the policeman. And whenever Padgett bellowed "Ball!" Joanna ran around in circles, scratching herself and then hiding her head under her arm as though to imply that she couldn't bear to watch such a brazen miscarriage of justice. The stand-up crowd that had gathered at the meadow began to titter; and Padgett, lobster-pink at the performance, glowered hostilely at his tormentor.

When the teams changed in the first inning, Abe Abelman, who played first for Franklinville, trotted down the base path with a broad grin.

"You fellows are going to lose either a mascot or an umpire," Abe told Sleepy.

The rival first baseman was a tall, good-humored boy whom Sleepy liked instantly. Dixie Bell, sports editor of the Culver City *Press,* had called Abe the best hitter in the Little League, and Northfield certainly had reason to stand in awe of Abe since two days previously he had hit a home run against Culver City's McGillicuddy.

"You must have had that guy's number," Sleepy said. Abe's homer had driven in three runs and given Franklinville the victory.

"We were in camp together last summer," Abe replied. "I always tag Mac on the same throw—his let-up pitch."

Sleepy, going on to the bench, stored away this information for future reference.

Buzz stuck to the same batting order he had used against Culver City, and Asphalt went to the plate to lead off for Northfield while Tennessee crouched in the batter's circle, waiting his turn. Padgett adjusted his mask as the sandy-haired Franklinville hurler completed his warm-up pitches.

"Put on those hitting shoes," sang out Buzz.

Asphalt responded with a stinging single. Tennessee doubled. Northfield indeed had donned its hitting shoes. By the time the inning ended the home nine had batted around to Turkey and four runs had crossed the plate. Another run was scored in the second and two more in the third. Franklinville, touted as even tougher than Culver City, was proving to be a push-over. Behind 7 to 0 with the game only half completed, the visitors called in a relief pitcher.

"That's the way it goes sometimes," Buzz said happily. "Everybody clicks!"

Meanwhile Turkey kept bearing down. Turkey's fast ball plunked into Poke's mitt with a solid, commanding thump, and his curve broke sharply. Sleepy wondered if the sight of Johnny pitching to Kelly in the grove at Echo Lake was responsible for Turkey's impressive exhibition. The old Turk was hot today, no matter what had ignited the fire in his pitching arm! Even the mighty Abe Abelman could manage no better than a scratch single against Turkey's biting slants.

"Hey," Abe prodded Sleepy, "why don't you apes warn a guy when you're going to get so uppity?"

"Who's the monkey now?" Sleepy shot back.

Abe laughed. "I guess we are. Well, if you dump us and if we dump Culver City, at least it'll all come out even."

For the moment, Sleepy was satisfied with that compromise.

With the game becoming so one-sided, the afternoon would have been spoiled entirely for the fans from Franklinville if it had not been for Joanna. From inning to inning the feud between Padgett and the Northfield mascot grew more heated. Sleepy, playing first, stood nearest to the end of the bench where Joanna, tugging on the chain held by Kelly, capered and hurled a monkey's brand of ridicule at the agitated umpire.

A climax to this state of unrest must come sooner or later. In the crowd of spectators behind the Northfield bench Sleepy noticed a news photographer, waiting patiently with camera and flashlight poised for the right moment of crisis.

At the plate the Franklinville players again struggled

vainly to connect with Turkey's deceptive pitches. Then a
Franklinville batter topped a slow curve and the ball trickled
between the mound and first.

The play at the base was certain to be close, and Padgett
charged down the path after the runner so that he would be
right on top of the throw. Turkey hustled after the ball,
seized it in his bare hand, and flipped to Sleepy. The Franklinville boy's foot came down on the bag.

"Safe!" roared Padgett.

Sleepy, sure he had taken the throw ahead of the runner,
protested strenuously.

With the traditional disdain of umpires, Padgett started
to walk away.

The policeman heard the crowd explode into an uproar.
He looked back. Behind him stood Joanna. No one ever
would be able to say whether it was by design or accident
that the monkey held her hands over her eyes. But the in-
ference was clear. The umpire, said Joanna's manner, was
sadly, dangerously blind!

Padgett whirled toward the Northfield bench.

"Get this Rhesus devil off the field," he snapped.

Joanna uncovered her eyes, stole a glance at Padgett,
then slapped her paws back over her face.

Kelly complained, "Aw, Padgett, if she goes I'll have to go
with her!"

Where earlier Padgett's countenance had looked lobster-
pink it now glowed turkey-red. He yanked out an enormous
pocket watch.

"One minute," he decreed thunderously. "Either you clear
that Joanna off the bench or Northfield loses this game by for-
feit!"

The news photographer stepped forward. His flash bulb

blazed. Within two hours a news syndicate was spreading from coast to coast the pictorial evidence of how, watch in hand, an umpire actually chased a monkey from a baseball game! In importance the picture quite overshadowed North-field's final 9-to-0 victory over Franklinville!

While the visiting players waited for the bus that would carry them home to Franklinville, Abe Abelman singled out Sleepy.

"Do you guys put on a show like this every game?"

"Not quite."

"This Buzz Kyler certainly has taught you guys a lot of baseball."

"Buzz is tops."

Abe twisted his foot in the grass. "Has Dixie Bell been down here?"

Sleepy felt a sudden tenseness, for his distrust of Dixie never had faded completely. "Yeah. Why?"

"Dixie and Buzz get along all right?"

"Sure."

"Well, then I guess Dixie was only making conversation that day he came to Franklinville."

Sleepy faced Abe. What was the rival first baseman trying to tell him? The roar of the Franklinville bus coming down the road seemed to fill Abe with relief.

"I'll be seeing you," he said. "And we'll pay back you fellows when we get a crack at you on our own ball field!"

Sleepy began, "About Dixie—"

"It wasn't really anything. You know how it is when time hangs on a fellow's hands and he takes to shooting the breeze."

Abe hurried toward the bus. Was the other boy simply ribbing to get back for the defeat Franklinville had suffered that afternoon? But Sleepy knew in his heart that Abe Abelman wasn't that kind of loser.

Next morning even the out-of-town newspapers reaching Northfield displayed prominently the picture of Padgett ordering Kelly and Joanna from the field. Aspects of that scene which had not been detected by every pair of eyes—including Padgett's—had not escaped the camera. Joanna's hands, it appeared, had been placed behind her ears in a most derisive and disrespectful gesture. And Kelly, shuffling beyond Padgett's line of vision, had expressed his rebellion by proceeding with tongue outstuck!

Sleepy, Lover, and Johnny stared at the photograph with an intermingling of awe and apprehension.

"You know," Lover said, "even among Irishmen there's a limit to how far you can stretch the bonds of friendship!"

"Gentlemen," agreed Sleepy, "never has a motivation for murder been clearer than the nose on Lover's face—and that's really hitting you with it!"

Johnny gulped. "If I may quote Kelly," he said, "I have only one word to say: faith!"

It did not reassure any of the boys, upon reaching the corner of Maple and Main, to discover that no Padgett had appeared to direct traffic from beneath the awninged stand.

"I think a meat cleaver is one weapon that will appeal to Padgett," Lover speculated. "On the other hand, there's much to be said for a sawed-off shotgun and a flame thrower."

"If Kelly has a choice," Sleepy conjectured, "I bet he'll want to fight it out with bulldozers at forty paces!"

"Winner to stuff the other's head as a fireplace decoration," said Lover, who began to see a variety of possibilities in the situation. "We might sell miniatures. Kids like Mr. Trouble would love 'em—we'd soon put Teddy bears off the market. Make nice stickpins too for the older folks, and—"

"Oh, shut up!" Johnny broke in. "This is serious. I don't want anything to happen to poor old Kelly."

"How about poor old Padgett?" Sleepy prodded. "After all, he's the one we can't find where he's supposed to be!"

"Let Padgett fend for himself," Johnny retorted. "He's got Mrs. Padgett to look out for him, but Kelly's all alone in the world!"

"Except for Joanna," said Lover.

"And Joanna's fleas," added Sleepy.

Johnny remained troubled, and his agitation mounted when, as the morning progressed, nowhere in Northfield was there a sign of either Padgett or Kelly. Both seemed to have evaporated with the morning mists—leaving, said Lover, whose poetic soul rose to the moment, "naught but their dying words whispered in the ear of a singing thrush!" Lover's imagination throbbed with the possibilities.

"Of course they've fought a duel. With casting lines and fishhooks." And Lover's squeaky voice imitated a radio sports announcer. "Zing! A fine cast by Kelly sinks a hook in Padgett's ear. There goes the pride of Northfield's police force, running out line, bobbing and twisting, a champion among human tuna. Zowie! Padgett hits back, conking Kelly on the noggin with an eight-ounce sinker. They've thrown away their rods and taken to crabbing nets. No, no—it's harpoons. Moby Dick is now the referee. Cautiously the two opponents close in on the edge of a tidal wave. Vultures are circling overhead. The pound of the surf is deafening. This epic struggle—brought to you by courtesy of Peerless Razors for the skin you love to peel—"

Even Johnny began to giggle.

But underneath Johnny remained worried, and so did

Sleepy, and by noon when still they could uncover no trace of Padgett or Kelly even the edge of Lover's jocular manner dulled. At lunch Mr. Jones took an offhand view toward the whole matter.

"There's a perfectly logical explanation to their disappearance."

"Like murder, I suppose," Sleepy said.

"Of course not! After all, they're both grown men!"

Mrs. Jones sniffed. "You can look at that picture in the paper and say that? Why, if you asked me, from the way they both acted they aren't any more grown up than Mr. Trouble, except that they both need shaves."

Sleepy grinned. "What's happened to that famous 'balance of power'?"

"Please don't be impudent," Mr. Jones rejoined with dignity. "*Thus far* our discussion doesn't involve *disciplining* you!"

Sleepy chuckled to himself.

When practice ended that afternoon no clues had developed to the whereabouts of Padgett or Kelly, and Buzz was as helpless as anyone to shed light upon the mystery. Lover, perhaps to bolster his own morale, took a new view of the situation.

"As I see it, it's the guy who took the picture that they're after! Once they've disposed of the corpse, so the crime is perfect, they'll be back putting up a brave front—"

"An' for what reason, would ye be so kind to say?" inquired Kelly's voice as he approached down the path.

Little Lover's eyes widened. With Kelly came Padgett, and both men *did* carry fishing rods! They carried also a string of pickerel and perch that attested to unusual proficiency at the sport of angling.

"A day's fishing will patch up any grievance," Kelly said. "The Irish are verra sensible in such matters. An' lucky we are to make it back in time so ye can each take a mess o' fish home to yer families!"

"Mind that you scale 'em for your mothers," said Padgett.

"With a Peerless Razor," suggested Lover. "For the skin you love to peel."

Sleepy drew a deep breath and risked the question on Kelly: "Have you or Padgett seen today's papers?"

"Why no, me lad. Is there something important?"

"Nothing that can't wait till morning," Buzz said quickly.

"Well, 'tis good 'tis that way. Right now Padgett an' I are so tuckered out we couldn't slap a mosquito!"

"You mean it?" Lover asked.

"Of course I mean it!"

"Indeed," agreed Padgett, yawning lustily.

"Then go look at the papers—right away," urged Lover, demonstrating that he was really a peace-loving boy at heart.

16 The
Glory Road

"LOVER," said Sleepy, "who slipped the thumb tack into the seat of your trousers? Honest, a guy with the seven-year itch couldn't be more impatient than you!"

"The bus won't wait," Lover insisted. "We've gotta get to Newton."

Sleepy sighed. Lover was right. Flushed with the victory over Franklinville, the whole Northfield team felt eager to tackle this second away game so that Newton's scalp could be added to its collection in the first round of the Little League competition.

"We're primed for this game," Lover burst out, as though he were a mind reader. "We'll mow 'em down!"

Still Sleepy hesitated, for reasons that were instantly obvious. Inside the Jones household arose a stentorian shout intended to be heard at least a mile away—an outburst from the remarkable lungs of Mr. Trouble:

"I wanna, wanna, *wanna!*"

"What," asked Lover appreciatively, for he was a connoisseur of voices with a far range, "does Mr. Trouble *wanna* do?"

"Go to the game."

"You can't blame him for that."

"It's not the game he cares about, but the ice cream cone he always gets. That guy's a shrewd little operator!"

"But aren't your mother and dad coming down to Newton for the game?"

In Lover's voice was the note of one who, faced with the evidence of high treason, still cannot quite believe it. Sleepy tried to hide his annoyance. The truth was that his mother, dad, and Mr. Trouble had planned on seeing the game; then, coming home from the store, Mr. Jones once more had experienced one of those silly cramps in his side as he had that afternoon at Echo Lake, and the family had decided to stay home so that he could rest. But Sleepy, more worried than he cared to confess, didn't see where this information was any concern of Lover's.

"Come on," he said shortly, as Mr. Trouble exploded with a new wail of misery. "We better make tracks!"

The doggone part of it, Sleepy reflected dismally as he hustled along Maple Avenue beside Lover, was the guilty notion that he was somehow responsible for his dad's trouble. Maybe if he gave up baseball and helped at the store . . .

"Newton, here we come," sang out Lover at the sight of the bus. "We'se gwine hit dat ole glory road!"

Sleepy grinned. Every time Lover knew how to ease a moment of tension. *The glory road*—that, by gosh, was exactly where the Northfield team was heading!

Culver City and Franklinville both had taken the measure of Newton in previous contests, however, and from the moment Buzz and his players disembarked at the field where the game would be played it became apparent from the remarks of the Newton boys that they were through being the doormat of the Little League.

"Don't underestimate this team," Buzz warned. "Unless I'm wrong they look to me as though they still had plenty of fight!"

Every team that they played, Sleepy thought, soon acquired its own mark of individuality. And yet, in a sense, this Newton team was different. At Culver City it had been McGillicuddy, the pitcher, who had been the spark—even to the point of his memory following them into the Tunnel of Love at Echo Lake. Abe Abelman, good-humored, a sportsman even in defeat, was the first image that sprang into Sleepy's mind when he remembered the game at Franklinville. But Newton impressed him more as just a team—a team that had been knocked down but didn't intend to stay down—and, in the long run, that sort of spirit might make Newton more dangerous than either Culver City or Franklinville. The large, enthusiastic home crowd exuded the same attitude, hollering and hooting on every play.

Three innings passed—fast, scoreless. Shad Rowe seemed to feel as Sleepy did. The Newton team, Shad proclaimed somewhat enviously, had the feeling of victory in its bones, and that was a tough thing to beat.

Lover, first at bat in the fourth, remained undaunted. Stopping at the water bucket on the way to the plate, he winked at Sleepy. "There's more than one way to skin a cat," he chuckled as he flipped the dipper back into the pail.

Lover's growing proficiency at bunting was earning him a well-deserved reputation. Now, cool and calculating, Lover waited until the count had gone to two balls and a strike before the bat moved from his shoulders. Then he dumped a bunt down the third base line and broke for first. Lover was at least a step ahead of the throw.

On the bench Buzz laughed. "Nothing puts a pitcher on edge as much as a neat bunt like that," he predicted.

A shift in the batting line-up sent Sleepy next to the plate, and he stood in the box, bat poised, feeling loose and confident. Lover danced down off first, chanting happily: "We's gwine hit dat ole glory road!" The Newton pitcher, clearly ruffled by Sleepy's calmness and Lover's antics, fidgeted with the rosin bag.

Into Sleepy's mind, as he waited, flashed Buzz's advice during that first batting practice: "Elbow straighter—elbow straighter!" Sleepy watched the pitch coming in—a slow, tantalizing curve—and pulled his arm up.

He knew that his timing would be right. Even as he swung, even before he felt the solid impact of bat against ball, his heart began to pound. He knew then—even before the left fielder turned and started to run, before Lover's scampering legs kicked up a dusty path around the bases, before the Northfield bench burst into a riotous cheer—that he was going to hit a home run! Just for an instant, after the bat connected, Sleepy watched the ball lifting. It seemed to take off like a frightened sparrow or peewee. And then it sailed straight up—and away!

A warm glow filled Sleepy as he circled the bases. On the mound the Newton pitcher watched in understandable dejection. And at home plate Buzz, Poke, Lover, Shad, and Kelly with Joanna on her chain were first to seize Sleepy's hand and to pound his back.

"As promised," Lover cried, thumping Sleepy's shoulder blades with the greatest vigor. "One cat skinned!"

Automatically Sleepy's eyes swept through the crowd, searching for his mother, father, and Mr. Trouble to see how they were enjoying his triumph; then he remembered why they were not there. The warm glow began to cool; a home run that he could not share with them did not seem so important as one he could. This glory road of Lover's could have its lonely spots!

But no one could deny that Sleepy's homer had fired the Northfield team. A double by Dodo Newson and a sizzling line single by Shad brought in another run before Newton finally decided to call in a relief pitcher.

"Looks like you started something," Buzz told the first baseman. And Buzz chuckled.

Sleepy's head inclined in a good-natured nod; part of the warm glow returned; but there also remained a remnant of the uneasy sense of guilt that he had felt while hurrying with Lover to catch the bus to Newton.

Working steadily behind a 3-to-0 lead, Turkey appeared well on the way to his second successive victory. With two outs in the fifth, however, the Newton catcher nicked Turkey for a double.

"Only a lucky bingle," Lover hooted derisively. "We'll get the next one easy."

Turkey nodded confidently. The batter who now faced him had grounded out previously on a slow curve, and Turkey had every intention of slow-curving the boy until he grew dizzy. Over-anxious, the batter once more topped Turkey's pitch and the ball bounded along the first base line.

Sleepy roused from his daydream. Just when—or how— he had started thinking about his father again he would never be able to say. But one thing was certain: he *hadn't* been concentrating on the batter.

Frantically, in the hope that amends might still be made, Sleepy charged the ball. He had started too late. His gloved hand reached down, but the ball wasn't there! Instead, his foot struck the grounder and bounced it toward the stands. Red-faced at the error, Sleepy chased after the ball, but the runner on second was safely home by the time Sleepy retrieved it. A fat lot of satisfaction he could take from his home run after ruining Turkey's shut-out! Some stuff, the glory road—take your mind off it one instant and you were dumped in a ditch!

Filled with remorse, Sleepy apologized to Turkey when the inning ended.

"Everyone boots one now and then," Turkey answered, and if a note of sulkiness crept into the pitcher's voice Sleepy couldn't much blame him.

Buzz glanced curiously at Sleepy, but said nothing. After all, Northfield still led 3 to 1, and the margin looked good enough to win. Actually Northfield added another run in its half of the sixth on successive singles by Tennessee, Lover, and Sleepy, and this extra insurance proved thoroughly unnecessary, for Turkey fanned the last three Newton batsmen to face him.

Spirits ran high on the bus ride back to Northfield. But Sleepy continued to brood—over the error, over the uneasy feeling that had motivated it. Buzz dropped down on the seat beside him.

"What's eating you, Sleepy?"

"Dad had another one of those funny attacks."

"Is that why your folks didn't come down for the game?"

"Yes."

Buzz looked out the window; across the road horses grazed in a meadow.

"Maybe I ought to give up baseball and help dad in the store," Sleepy blurted. "All the time—except when I'm in school."

"Does your dad want you to?" Buzz asked.

"I—I never put it to him straight out."

"Afraid he might say yes?"

"I guess so."

Buzz smiled. "Well, you haven't much choice now, Sleepy. You've faced up to your conscience and you'll have to go through with it. Ask him what he wants you to do."

Sleepy nodded. Just for an instant he felt choked at the thought that this might be the last time all summer he'd be riding back from a game with the team, and then the sense of regretfulness passed. He had to know where he stood with his dad. He wouldn't be of much good to anybody unless he knew once and for all that he wasn't letting his father down.

When the bus stopped at the Northfield depot, Buzz spoke again to Sleepy.

"It was a peach of a homer, Sleepy."

"Thanks."

"And it did wake up the whole team."

"Lover's bunt did that."

Buzz held out his hand and Sleepy clasped it.

"Chin up," the coach said.

Sleepy guessed that it would be difficult to find anyone who, underneath, was more regular than Buzz Kyler.

Maple Avenue was quiet when Sleepy bounded along the street, falling into the childish habit of skipping over the cracks in the superstition that to step on one was to break somebody's back. When the boy reached home, he found his dad sitting in the porch swing. Beside the man sat Mr.

Trouble, sucking on the old blue crib blanket that was the three-year-old's constant source of comfort in moments of relaxation.

"How did the game go?" Mr. Jones asked.

Sleepy described Northfield's 4-to-1 victory over Newton, adding offhandedly, "In the fourth I hit a homer!"

Mr. Jones did not disguise his pride and excitement. "Sleepy, you got hold of one, eh? That was dandy!"

Even Mr. Trouble sensed the importance of his brother's feat, and broke off his blanket sucking. "Sleepy run home! Sleepy run home!"

Mr. Jones laughed. "Your brother has the words mixed, but his heart certainly is in the right place."

Sleepy shuffled his foot across the floor of the porch. "Then I pulled an awful boner," he said. Awkwardly—for it was a hard confession to make—he told about the error and why it had been committed. Two tiny spots of red burned above Sleepy's high cheekbones when he finished. "Dad," he said, "you've got to tell me. Am I letting you down?"

If Mr. Jones's nose suddenly had erupted with the year's worst itch, he couldn't have rubbed it more vigorously.

"Far from it," he said. "Far, far from it!"

"If it means giving up baseball—"

Mr. Jones said: "I can manage the store, Sleepy. After all, I'm still a grown man. And you boys have sort of made a contract with the merchants of Northfield to give them the best team you possibly can in the Little League. I think you've got to live up to that obligation, Sleepy—especially when you can do it with a home run now and then!"

"I'll never hit another."

"Don't be too sure of that!"

The relief, the quiet feeling of pride that gave Sleepy a

sudden tingling sensation was not easily described. But, as Buzz had said, not only had he faced up to his conscience but he had been willing to accept whatever the consequences must be, and now there needn't be any more silly daydreaming when a shut-out was at stake! Self-conscious in his personal triumph, Sleepy beheld Mr. Trouble sucking on his blanket.

"You can't tell what sort of diseases he could pick up from that thing," the older boy said critically.

Mr. Jones smiled. "We all need a crutch to lean on now and then," the man advised. "That's why 'live and let live' is a pretty happy philosophy of life. And I daresay supper's almost ready, so shall we go in for once before mother has to call us?"

With one arm around Sleepy and another around Mr. Trouble, Mr. Jones led his two sons into the house.

17 Low
and Mean

ANOTHER GAME with Culver City loomed on Northfield's schedule, and the memories of both the previous defeat by this team and of McGillicuddy's finesse as a pitcher gave a grim note to practice the following day despite Northfield's recent victory over Newton.

At Sleepy's appearance at practice, Buzz grinned.

"So you weren't as big a heel as you thought?" the ex-Yankee chuckled.

"So it seems."

Buzz's eyes softened. "You did the right thing, Sleepy—a difficult thing—and yet because you did do it you'll be a better player. There has to be character in baseball, too."

Sleepy felt a little foolish—and immensely pleased. Buzz continued:

"You were lucky, too. You see, I had to face up to whether I was letting down the fans, and to admit that I was. Until you boys came along I had no choice but to quit baseball forever!"

Mr. Baseball, thought Sleepy. Every inch of Buzz gave

something to the game and made it vital and worthy of a fellow's best effort.

It was to be an afternoon of many surprises. First among them was Kelly, who tugged a protesting Joanna on her chain.

" 'Tis luck this old flea-cage is supposed to bring us," Kelly announced, "an' who am I to snoot a sensible superstition?"

"Like walking under ladders, I suppose," Lover demanded.

"That, too. Especially when there's someone on the ladder who may not like ye with a bucket o' paint he may dump on yer head. Mind ye, 'tis only *sensible* superstitions I'm speakin' of."

"And why are you so anxious to court all this luck?" Lover persisted.

"That," said Kelly, with the air of mystery to which he was devoted, "is something ye'll see in the sweet by an' by."

Joanna hissed and pulled back, but Kelly was a stubborn man and he yanked resolutely until the pair reached the bench. Here he spread himself in comfort, scratching Joanna's ear and feeding her a lump of sugar as consolation for the annoyance he had caused her. Upon Kelly's countenance was an expression of happy expectancy—a bad sign, thought Sleepy, for the last time Kelly had so disported himself he had ruined the morals of a good portion of Northfield's canine and feline populations.

Practice had started before Kelly's secret was revealed. Then through the path where once Poke's Pipe Dream had been erected to snare the wayward Joanna appeared Johnny Kyler. He carried a fielder's glove and wore a Northfield uniform.

"Can you use another batting practice pitcher?" he asked, hiding his embarrassment behind a hint of bravado.

Johnny's presence, and Johnny's uniform, obviously were all Kelly's doing, for no one more than Buzz seemed caught by surprise. But even the note of gruffness that Buzz assumed could not disguise his pleasure.

"Sure—sure," Buzz said. "This is open season on batting practice pitchers around here."

Buzz waved Dodo Newson away from the plate so that Johnny could unlimber with a few warm-up pitches to Poke.

The new recruit looked pitifully self-conscious in his debut on the mound, and his first few throws were gentle lobs intended to loosen his arm. Every pair of eyes followed the flight of the ball as it passed between Johnny and Poke, but Kelly's gaze was the most intense.

"If only he can begin to sweat," the Irishman muttered. "Then I'll know he really feels free an' easy."

Johnny began to bear down. Sleepy, watching, thought that Johnny's fast ball still stayed too high with too much tendency to float instead of spanking down toward the plate, but there could be no doubt that in the two weeks since the excursion to Echo Lake Johnny's curve had acquired more bite.

"That stuff breaks fast," Tennessee Martin commented respectfully.

But it was Johnny's low pitches that won most attention. The boy had developed a slider that began to fall away about halfway to the plate, and came in right across the knees of the average batter. It was the sort of pitch that drove Poke to his own knees to hold onto it, but the chunky catcher didn't appear to mind the dirt and every time his mitt was there echoing to the solid thump of the ball.

"That can be mean to hit," Dodo Newson said.

"And mean to catch," appended Asphalt Smith, who at

last had come to realize that his own famous inshoot-out-shoot was entirely a creation of his imagination.

Buzz sent Dodo back to the plate. Johnny walked him. Then Tennessee caught an outside curve for an authoritative single. It was true that Turkey struck out on a low pitch, but this feat scarcely ranked with the unusual achievements of baseball, for even Asphalt reckoned on restoring his confidence by occasionally fanning the old Turk. On the bench Kelly frowned as his fingers idly scratched Joanna's ear. Johnny still hadn't started to sweat.

"He's wound up tight like a drumhead," Kelly grumbled.

"What did you expect his first day out?" Lover asked.

"I suppose, I suppose." Kelly, however, could not conceal his disappointment. "He's better than he's showing."

"There's still two-thirds of the season to go," Lover pointed out.

Kelly's expression said: "Whoever expects an Irishman to be patient?" Did the change in effectiveness of Johnny's pitching when he was or was not facing a batter console Turkey, Sleepy wondered. Time would tell how insurmountable an obstacle this factor might be; meanwhile the North-field team had discovered a relief hurler who gave promise of developing. That circumstance could not help but build morale.

"As I see it," Shad Rowe told Sleepy, "if we had had Johnny when the season opened we might have beaten Culver City and be leading the Little League at this very moment!"

Buzz looked satisfied when Johnny finished his first stint on the mound. Johnny had come back to baseball, and in that triumph of personal spirit, Buzz's attitude suggested, was the real hope for the future.

Next morning Sleepy was pushing the lawn mower across the Jones back yard when Lover appeared, wanting to go down to the Y for a swim.

"So they stuck you again, eh?" chirped Lover sympathetically. "More orders from above?"

Sleepy shook his head. "This is my own idea—to help dad."

"How long will it take?"

"I ought to clip the hedge, too."

Lover shuffled awkwardly. It was hot and he wanted that swim. But he wanted it with Sleepy. "Where are your confounded clippers?" he decided at last. "If we clean up this job together there'll still be time for a short dip."

"Unless Joanna escapes again and interrupts us."

"Then Johnny and Kelly can darn well chase her," Lover declared. "We're going to get that swim!"

Sleepy badgered the lawn mower down the side of the yard. Behind him he could hear the snip of the clippers where Lover worked on the hedge. Times had changed all right. A summer ago each boy would have gone his own way, but now they were teammates who shared the bad breaks with the good. Buzz had taught them something, Sleepy thought, and if he must give a name to what that something was maybe it was nothing more spectacular than the mere process of growing up. Two hours later when with damp hair and open sports shirts the two boys came from their swim at the Y, Lover said: "I enjoyed that splash. By gosh, I worked for it!"

Again, Sleepy reflected, there was a grown-up tone in Lover's remark. A comfortable, grown-up tone.

Once more Kelly brought Joanna to practice. And that afternoon the Irishman's persistency in wooing Lady Luck promised quick returns. By the time Johnny completed his

warm-up pitches he was sweating freely. A cynic might have
ascribed this circumstance to the merciless July sun blazing
overhead, but Kelly was more the optimist feeling that with
the discomfiture of Johnny's debut behind him the boy had
begun to build confidence in being on the mound.

"Now ye'll see, now ye'll see," predicted Kelly, who appeared to be drifting into Mr. Trouble's habit of saying
everything twice.

Tennessee Martin, who had been the first to hit Johnny
solidly at the previous practice, had become a symbol in
the pitcher's mind. At the sight of Tennessee's long legs striding toward the plate Johnny frowned, and reached for the
rosin bag. Johnny's whole manner was one suggesting that
he wished to cause the slightest interruption possible in Tennessee's quest for a new four-leaf clover record; but at the
same time Johnny bore no personal grudge against Tennessee. Rather, his problem was to mow down Tennessee as an
example of what the other batters on the team might
expect!

Kelly leaned forward tensely, sensing the importance of
the drama about to unfold, and his eagerness was trans-
mitted even to Joanna for the Rhesus sat quietly at his feet.
Behind the plate Poke called softly: "Take this one in stride,
Johnny. There's nothing to fanning this tired old work
horse!"

Sleepy grinned. That Poke was a catcher to his toenails!

Johnny's fast ball stayed high and Tennessee waited, bat
on shoulder, giving the impression that all he needed was
patience to get on base the easy way. But the next pitch
bit in sharply, a fine curve, for a called strike, and Poke sang
out cheerfully, "He must have a little dust in his eyes,
Johnny. He can't seem to see 'em!"

Johnny went back to the rosin bag. Clearly he wanted to get the next pitch across and jump ahead of the batter by a two-to-one count. Beads of perspiration glistened on Johnny's forehead as he stepped onto the mound for his wind-up. Beads of perspiration also glistened on Tennessee's forehead as he braced himself in the batter's box for the low ball that was almost a certainty now.

"Here she comes," breathed Kelly. The words seemed to emerge in a gulp.

Johnny overtried. His arm was tight, his fingers jerky. His control was lost. The ball came in low, striking hard in front of the plate, skipping up . . .

Poke, down on his knees, tried to smother the ball. His mitt didn't touch it. Then Poke was flat on the ground, flat and limp. The ball, smacking with a thud against the catcher's head above his mask, careened crazily toward the bench.

Blood oozed from the cut high on Poke's temple.

Everyone rushed toward the plate, and Buzz, standing straddle-legged over the stricken catcher, shouted harshly, "Keep back! Give the kid air!" And to Lover the coach said tensely, "Go for a doctor—on the double quick!"

Sleepy, looking down aghast, hoped Poke would show some sign of consciousness, but the fat boy remained perfectly still. A bump the size of an egg had started rising on his head.

Tennessee swallowed audibly. "Gosh, he got it all right. Like being hit by a truck. We could afford to lose almost anybody on the team more than poor old Poke."

It was true, Sleepy admitted. Poke was so good that you simply took his presence for granted. But not to have Poke playing—

On this staggering thought Lover returned with Dr. Harrison. The medical man examined Poke for a full five minutes, swabbing his wound, and listening to his heart and pulse. Then Dr. Harrison said, "I suspect he has a mild concussion. An x-ray will tell. Anyhow, he'll come around in a moment and then we'll get him home. He's going to want to rest quietly all by himself to forget the awful headache he'll have."

Buzz said dismally, "It was just one of those things that sometimes are part of baseball."

"And part of life," Dr. Harrison added.

Sleepy saw Johnny's face then. White. Lower lip trembling. Eyes filled with self-blame.

"It wasn't your fault," Sleepy said.

Briefly Johnny met the first baseman's gaze, but he preferred to look away. "Wasn't it? *Maybe if you thought what it was like to catch a pitch like that you'd never throw it!*" Johnny stuffed his glove into his hip pocket. "More to the point, *maybe you'd never throw any pitch!*"

"But—but," Sleepy began when from over his shoulder Kelly's voice interrupted.

"Sleepy, there's a time to argue an' a time not. If ye're wise ye'll take an old man's advice. I know."

18 Poking Along

"NOTHING could be easier," Poke Johnson said, "than explaining my downfall. I am not a complicated fellow. Some guys need wine, women, and song to ruin their lives, but not me. Just once I take my eye off the ball and get conked on the head. What a dope!"

With the bandages that Dr. Harrison had wrapped over Poke's injury, the corpulent catcher looked like a turbaned sultan. His throne chair was the Northfield bench at the Culver City game, and, with legs wrapped around the sides of the water bucket, he continued his royal address:

"Doc says I'll be back playing in a couple of weeks— maybe for the next game against Franklinville. There's lots of good hard bone in my head. It's a big advantage."

Poke assumed full responsibility for the accident. It was a catcher's job, he maintained, to be able to handle a low ball that went wild, and when he muffed one he deserved to roll over with the other daisies.

"Now that Poke," Kelly told Sleepy, "would be a credit to any race—even the Irish."

"But no more so than Lover Carmichael," Sleepy said.

"Aye, me lad, 'tis true, 'tis true . . ."

In the minds of both man and boy lingered the memory of the practice following Poke's beaning. Waiting for Buzz, they had stood around in a listless, bewildered group, wondering how a baseball team functioned without a catcher. The image of Poke, flat and limp on the ground, had haunted each of them. "A guy could knock himself out for good that way," Tennessee Martin had grumbled, and the soberness of his countenance had not been lightened by his discovery, at that instant, of his eighteenth four-leaf clover of the season. Then down the path to the meadow had walked Buzz and Lover. In Poke's mask and chest protector, Lover had the awesome appearance of a visitor from Mars. With an extravagant bow, Lover had swept the grass with his mask and exclaimed, "Gentlemen, a star is born!"

Now, looking out from the bench to where Lover was handling Turkey's warm-up pitches, Sleepy grinned. On the basis of ability Lover was certainly no Poke as a catcher, but his spunk and spirit had saved the team's morale.

"He doesn't do bad," Poke said. "Anyhow, catching is mostly sticking up your mitt and hoping the ball will be there, and Lover's all right at that!"

Turkey, beginning to bear down, unloosed a fast ball that Lover caught easily. Whether Lover could display the same gracefulness in handling Turkey's deliveries when there was a Culver City batter at the plate or a Culver City runner on base would be a riddle that could only be known under actual game conditions, Sleepy thought.

Win or lose, the crowd was with Northfield today.

"Everybody likes to see the underdog bite back," Buzz said practically. "It's an old American custom."

Johnny sat next to Kelly, watching intently every move Lover made. Poke's good-humored acceptance of the accident, Lover's voluntary service as a substitute catcher, had helped Johnny some; but within his mind there were pictures of how much worse everything might have been.

"You enjoy torturing yourself," Poke said bluntly.

"You were lucky—and so was I."

"And I'm going to stay lucky, if I don't—" But Poke's voice trailed off, as though afraid to finish the sentence, and Kelly looked round sharply.

Johnny, lips pressed tight, prodded the catcher: "If you don't what?"

"Turn quitter!"

"You think I have?"

"I think you can."

Johnny's face reddened, and Kelly, always over-solicitous where Buzz's son was concerned, also flushed. But it was Buzz who spoke. "Kelly, I can't find the scorebook. Will you have a look for it?"

Sleepy felt his heart leap. Buzz's request to Kelly was obviously a pretense to get the Irishman out of the way. Buzz's instincts as a coach had overruled his instincts as a father, for if Johnny ever were to amount to anything to the team he must meet the challenge with which Poke faced him.

Johnny said, "That's a nasty crack."

"Only if it happens to be true," Poke answered.

"The team doesn't really need me."

"That remains to be seen."

"Then let the future take care of itself."

Poke fussed with the dipper in the water bucket. "I wasn't thinking too much about the future, but about this afternoon. We may need you in this game."

No scorebook ever had been found in better time than Kelly now displayed, but even so he was too late. Johnny blinked. The possibility that his services might be called upon in the Culver City game never had occurred to him, and the prospect clearly staggered him. Poke's steady glance remained stoical. Was Johnny a quitter or wasn't he?

Unthinkingly, Johnny wiped a hand across his forehead, and his fingers came away moist with perspiration. Poke went on.

"If it hadn't been for that bad break—if that low pitch had come in right—I think that you would have fanned Tennessee. You'd have been on your way as a pitcher."

"You had me scared," Tennessee confessed.

Johnny wet his lips. What he might have said no one ever knew, for at that moment Lover appeared with the announcement that Turkey was ready. "Primed like a hunk of first-class beef," said Lover. "Still, those Culver City batters are going to find the old Turk mighty tough chewing!"

Turkey wiped his face on a towel.

Buzz said: "Here comes the ump. You fellows better get out onto the field."

Lover replaced his mask. "This one is for Poke," he declared. "We're sort of poking along, you might say. Let's win it for him!"

Poke's happy expression said that, win or lose, Lover was all right with him. Johnny looked away and his eyes still blinked. Was he wondering if in a pinch he'd prove all right with Poke? Did he care?

Sleepy, trotting off to first, felt that Johnny did care, but the big problem just then was Lover and not Johnny. Likely Culver City would bunt until Lover blew wide open or demonstrated that he was not as much of a ham, second-string catcher as the circumstances suggested. Baseball games, like wars, could be won on the other fellow's weakness as well as on your own strength. Lover's gesture had been noble, but this was the moment, the game, the pay-off!

Whipping the ball across the infield, kicking first to make sure the bag was securely pegged, feeling the excitement of the crowd around him, Sleepy drew a deep breath. There must be five hundred at the game, and, he wagered, Mr. Trouble alone remained calm. Mr. Trouble, as usual, was busily discoloring his chin with a dripping ice cream cone.

Lover had anticipated the bunt, but he was overanxious as the ball trickled toward third. Suddenly Lover seemed to support three feet instead of two and to be wearing a mitt on both his hands. By the time Lover, ruddy with embarrassment, had extricated himself from these difficulties of fact and fancy and grabbed the ball, the Culver City batsman rested safely on first.

"Sorry, Turk," Lover said tightly, and yanked on his mask.

Lover looked grim, but grimness didn't win baseball games, Sleepy reflected. He held the base against the runner, hopeful for a pick-off play, but the other boy watched cautiously. After all, another bunt for Lover to boot would put him on second. Why run a risk?

Turkey swallowed uncomfortably. He, too, was under a strain.

Again, the bunt. Again, Lover found that he possessed too many feet. But the ball this time came toward first, and Sleepy charged it. "This one is for Poke—and for Lover," he thought.

Ball, runner, Sleepy appeared to converge on the same point. But Sleepy never broke stride. Bending low, he scooped for the ball. His hand came up and made the tag. Then, spinning, he pegged for second. The runner from first went into the bag head-first, hands outstretched, a belly-whopper. Dust kicked up in a cloud.

But Sleepy had the same feeling now as when he had hit the home run against Newton. He knew the ball would be there ahead of the runner. The double play had wiped out both ends of the Culver City threat!

There was a special pleasure for Sleepy in the cheer that burst from the Northfield rooters. This time his mother and dad were there to share his triumph, and the warm glow could linger. When almost at once the cheer turned into peals of laughter, the reason why was understandable: Poke, overjoyed, had plunged his foot in the water bucket when he tried to jump up. The fat boy's turbaned head and bucketed foot eased even Lover's tenseness.

In a sense, history had repeated itself. Who but Lover had placed them under a strain in the first Culver City game, and how had Northfield emerged from that crisis except through a double play? Now, as then, Turkey settled down, getting a fast break into his curve, and whiffing the next batter even though the boy tried twice to connect for a bunt.

But history played no favorites. McGillicuddy proved no less effective than when last he had pitched against Northfield. Three batters faced him and were out on futile infield rollers. The pity of the thing, Poke groaned, was the fact that they hadn't found McGillicuddy's corpse in the Tunnel of Love.

If stubbornness were a virtue, Sleepy soon came to decide, the least that could be said for the Culver City coach was that he promised some day to become a saint. He sent his team to the plate in the second with the same instructions that he had given them in the first—to bunt Lover crazy.

Lover snugged down his mask and glowered ferociously at the batsman who waited now for Turkey's first pitch. When the ball came in, up went the bat of the Culver City boy. Lover catapulted forward, eyes fixed on the skittering ball. He snatched it and whirled. Why, doggone, it could be easy! His throw would nip the runner by two full strides!

"You're next," Lover chirped cheerfully to the next Culver City batter. "You guys can't bunt—not even against a dumb catcher like me!"

The Culver City lad looked toward the bench, wondering if the bunt signal had been switched. Turkey wiped his face and squeezed the rosin bag. Sleepy kicked at first base. In both their minds was the same question: had Lover been lucky or had he really risen above the reign of terror with which the Culver City bunters intended to annihilate him? From the Northfield bench Poke called encouragingly, "On your toes, Lover! Nothin' to it if you just watch the ball!"

The Culver City coach remained unconvinced, and the bunt signal was unchanged. This time the batter hit a teaser—a mean, twisting grounder between third and the pitcher's mound that invited the catcher, pitcher, and third baseman to crack their skulls converging on it. Lover went after the ball as though it were a football, grabbing it in a head-long dive. Rolling over on his knees, Lover threw hard to first. And across the diamond roared the umpire's lusty shout: *"Out!"*

Sleepy pulled his foot off the base and watched the disappointed Culver City runner puff by. There wasn't any luck in that play except the luck that Lover had produced by his own hustling! By gosh, when it came to picking an all-county team at the end of the summer no one in the Little League—not even Culver City's McGillicuddy or Franklinville's Abe Abelman—would have any better claim to that honor than Lover! His real nickname should be Mr. Emergency, for he was the boy who came through whenever the going grew roughest!

The next Culver City batter swung mightily and lifted a towering fly that Dodo Newson caught in short left. Lover chuckled.

"Ended," Lover told Buzz, flopping down on the bench, "one epidemic of buntitis."

"Except for a couple of bunts you may yet hit yourself," Buzz answered, also chuckling.

Johnny regarded Lover with unconcealed admiration. "That guy's got it all right," he muttered to Kelly.

"Aye, an' 'tis a nice thing to have," Kelly said. "A backbone."

Johnny stared down at the grass, kicking the ground with a worrisome scowl and not realizing that he trampled one of the four-leaf clovers on which Tennessee's bid for fame depended.

Meanwhile history, once falling into the habit of repeating itself, seemed rather to enjoy that experience. The score board in center field began to tell a story familiar to those who had attended the first game with Culver City:

Team	1	2	3	4	5	6	R	H	E
Culver City	0	0	0	0	0				
Northfield	0	0	0	0					

Poke's marks in history at school might not be the best, but Poke's knowledge of history where baseball was affected carried authority. Lover and Tennessee would be second and third at bat in the fifth, and if either nicked McGillicuddy for a hit the batsman would be Turkey.

"Only a fool would let history repeat itself that much," Poke said. "If you're wise, Johnny, you'll start to warm up."

Johnny gulped. "*Me?*"

"Uh-huh," Poke said unfeelingly. "I wouldn't be surprised if you might be called on to do double duty—to pinch-hit for Turkey and then to relieve for him!"

"But—but—"

"But, my eye! Everybody knows you would have fanned Tennessee except for a fluke. If you want to pull yourself together, you can make it—at least for the short stint on which this game may hang!"

Johnny's neck itched almost as badly as though he had just sat in a barber's chair. "But Poke, this is a big game—"

"In the won or lost column in the league standings they're all the same size," Kelly cut in. "Come on, I'll warm ye up!"

And Kelly fairly lifted Johnny to his feet. The boy's face

was pale as he suffered himself to be led away to the clear space behind the backstop.

Poke glanced across at Buzz and grinned. "Think it's worth the gamble?"

Buzz nodded. "Like Lover," the coach said, "I'm willing to poke along this game!"

19 The Pay-Off

SLEEPY suddenly wished that he owned two pairs of eyes. Trying at the same time to watch Dodo Newson at the plate and Kelly warming up Johnny behind the backstop gave the first baseman's head the feeling of being the shuttlecock in a badminton game. Dodo proved to be an unrewarding spectacle; with the count at two balls and two strikes, Dodo reached for an outside pitch and trickled a feeble grounder toward shortstop for an easy out.

Dodo returned to the bench, disgusted with himself. "That McGillicuddy's tough," he grumbled, voicing the afternoon's most unnecessary remark.

Poke grunted, but his eyes were on the Culver City infield as Lover walked up to the plate. "They've got that guy's number now," the injured catcher complained. "Look how the infielders move up automatically two or three steps in anticipation of a bunt."

"Who says he has to bunt?" Buzz asked.

To everyone's surprise, Lover swung solidly on McGillicuddy's first pitch. His bat caught hold of enough of the ball to lift a soft liner into short right, the perfect spot for a clean single with the Culver City infield pulled in.

Poke wanted to laugh. "You could say history did or did not repeat, depending on whether you referred to Lover being on base or his method of getting there."

Buzz called Tennessee back from the plate. "Wait out McGillicuddy as long as you can," the Northfield coach said. "Johnny needs every warm-up pitch we can give him."

Sleepy forgot Tennessee temporarily. His eyes held fast to Johnny's long, gangling kick as he brought his arm over and whipped the ball into Kelly's glove. Sleepy hoped that Johnny had begun to sweat; yet, in all fairness, he had to admit that the boy was being called on short notice to prove his mettle. Both literally and figuratively, he had become Johnny-on-the-spot! Then, fleetingly, Sleepy caught a glimpse of Turkey's face: grim, sullen, resentful. Well, whose fault was it that Turkey remained the weakest hitter on the squad? And even if the old Turk's pride had been pricked, which came first—Turkey's tender sensibilities or the good of the team? Anyhow, Turkey had done his part—he had held together during those critical first innings when Culver City had tried to bunt Lover into blowing up—and how much glory did Turkey need for one afternoon?

McGillicuddy was no fool and could guess not only why Johnny was warming up but also why Tennessee wanted to stay at bat as long as he could. The natural competitor in McGillicuddy, the fighting streak that made everyone respect him, explained his sudden flush. His first pitch stayed high, but then he broke two fast curves right across the letters on Tennessee's chest. This was pitching in the clutch with muscle, brain, and heart, and the crowd cheered. Tennessee gripped his bat, really sweating now if Johnny wasn't.

With two called strikes he couldn't afford to ignore anything that even resembled a good pitch.

"I feel," Poke said, "as though I had just eaten an old shoe."

McGillicuddy gave Tennessee a fast ball. The Northfield batter swung too soon and the ball, plunking into the catcher's mitt, supplied a dull accompaniment to the umpire's booming: "Str-rike three. *Yer out!*"

Lover was there first.

The catcher bobbed up, arm pulled back. Lover hadn't waited—Lover's scampering legs carried him down the path toward second. The ball whistled across the infield and Lover dove. The second baseman's glove reached down. But Lover was there first. Everyone knew it. Lover had stolen second and was in scoring position!

"I just digested that old shoe," Poke announced gleefully.

"Well, you're about to swallow another," Buzz told him crisply, and stood up to motion Johnny in to pinch-hit for Turkey. Buzz walked down to speak to his son at the bat rack. He said: "Don't try to kill the ball—simply meet it."

Then Buzz came back to the bench. Almost as superstitious as Kelly, the coach crossed his fingers.

When Johnny was announced as the pinch hitter, the Culver City catcher said sarcastically: "So you're another Kyler? Well, you can be sure of this much—you're about to make even a faster fadeout than your old man did!"

Johnny backed out of the batter's box, ostensibly to dust his hands so that he could grip the bat more firmly, but actually he was fighting for self-control. Nothing obscured a fellow's batting eye like a flash of temper.

McGillicuddy stretched and looked down at the plate. The catcher's taunting voice continued.

"They tell me your old man knocked down most of the fences in the minor leagues—butting 'em with his head when he tried to catch the ball!"

He'd take a swipe at the first pitch that came anywhere near the plate, Johnny decided. There was a limit to how much of this ribbing he could take before his anger exploded. The catcher went on: "They tell me—"

The ball came in, fast and high. Johnny dug his toes into

the dirt and swung. The end of the bat connected. Lover started for third, running low to the ground like a hare chased by a hound. The ball soared on a line across the infield, and the Culver City second baseman raced back, leaping frantically. His outstretched fingertips couldn't reach the drive. Johnny crossed the bag at first as the centerfielder scooped up the ball on the first bounce. And Lover, rounding third, pounded on toward home.

A turban-headed Poke flung his arms around Kelly's neck. "Ja see that, Kelly? He smacked it! We're ahead!"

"Aye, I saw it," the Irishman replied. "An' 'twas something, me lad . . . 'twas something indeed!"

Buzz said: "Don't count your chickens too soon. Culver City still has a turn at bat!"

Puffing after the score, Lover dropped down on the grass beside Sleepy. The big 1 that went up on the scoreboard after Northfield's name looked wonderful. Now if they could hold onto that lead, the season's most unexpected upset would be theirs!

"If you're a praying man, pray now," Lover advised Sleepy between gulps for breath.

"I'm praying all right," Sleepy answered.

But even prayer couldn't help Shad in advancing Johnny beyond first. McGillicuddy settled down grimly to the business of ending an inning in which he had been handled with undeserved roughness on Lover's steal of second and Johnny's hit on a bad pitch. Shad suffered the blazing aftermath of the pitcher's pique. Shad swung mightily, but every time the ball was past before his bat came around.

"Here we go," chirped Lover, buckling on his leg protectors. "We can't do any worse than lose—and we can win!"

Poke waddled over to home plate with Lover. Johnny met them there.

"I take it back," Poke said. "You're no quitter!"

"Don't be too sure—yet."

"I am sure," Poke insisted. "And if you'll take my advice, you won't try any fancy stuff. Let Lover hold up his mitt and aim for it. Just blaze 'em in. You can get by now on speed. They're on edge."

Johnny nodded.

"A dozen of the right pitches and it can all be over!"

Again Johnny nodded.

Sleepy's prayers, having failed with Shad, were transferred to Johnny. Just let him sweat, Sleepy's mind pleaded. Lover crouched behind the plate, mitt elevated for a target. On the mound Johnny swung his arm upward and rocked back for his first pitch.

The ball sang—a white streak that cut across the plate and plunked into Lover's glove. The catcher pulled out his hand and shook it gingerly. Despite the heavy padding of the mitt that pitch had stung. But Lover simply grinned and called out, "Burn it in again, Johnny! If the grass catches on fire we'll organize a bucket brigade!"

Johnny caught Lover's return throw and bounced the ball in his glove.

Sleepy called, "You're on that old glory road, Johnny!"

On the Northfield bench Kelly sat hunched over, his head almost lost behind his knees, as though afraid to watch.

But Johnny neither heard nor saw. The anger was rising in him. So that's what they said—Buzz had butted down the minor league fences with his head! So that's what they thought—he was a fadeout like Buzz! Dimly, behind the plate, the boy recognized Lover's mitt, raised and waiting.

But Johnny still bounced the ball in his glove. Poke had spoken sensibly. Speed could do it. A dozen right pitches were all he needed—maybe only nine or ten more now! Johnny wiped a hand across his forehead. Then he looked down at the hand, feeling better at the moist streaks of dirt.

He had begun to sweat like an overworked mule!

Sleepy, counting the pitches that Johnny threw, thought no poetry ever had contained a prettier rhythm. On Number Four the first Culver City batsman returned dejectedly to the bench; on Number Seven that unhappy lad was joined by Johnny's second strike-out victim; and on Number Ten Northfield stood one strike away from victory and the Little League lead.

Lover realized that a hush had descended on the crowd. If anybody had wanted to drop a pin, Lover said afterward, it would have been heard. Lover held up his mitt and taunted the batter: "Close your eyes, kid—it'll be easier to bear!"

Actually the Culver City boy *did* close his eyes. The umpire's hand snapped back to indicate the last strike and Sleepy broke for the mound to fling his arms around Johnny's shoulders. But Buzz and Kelly reached there first, unmindful of Poke's frantic imprecations to wait for him. Once more the fat boy had jammed his foot in the water bucket. There was a giddiness in the cheers that at last rocketed across the field.

No one summed up the spirit of the moment more cogently than Dixie Bell in his story in the Culver City *Press* the following afternoon:

> The joy so long delayed broke loose, and with good reason: no
> major league game ever had packed more thrills and more heart-

breaks in six innings than this Little League contest between Culver City and Northfield . . .

Further down the column Sleepy found himself mentioned by name:

> . . . Sleepy Jones—the lad who hit the home run just a week ago against Newton—was the big hero to this reporter. In the first inning, when Northfield's cause looked rockier than your grandmother's favorite porch chair, he initiated the fielding gem of the day, a double play that reversed the tide completely. When it comes to doling out individual all-county honors at the end of the summer, it should be all but impossible to overlook the claim that Sleepy already has staked . . .

All-county! All the distrust that Sleepy ever had felt toward Dixie Bell was dispelled by the warmth that filled his heart. After all, looking back, he guessed that double play had been the turning point!

Mr. Jones read the story more soberly. The man shook his head. "Dixie isn't much of a reporter if you're the only one he singles out."

Sleepy felt hurt. "Gosh, I didn't ask him—"

"Of course you didn't," Mr. Jones said. "Your double play was fine, but only proportionally so. It was part of a truly great game—but so was Poke's spirit on the bench, and Lover's play on that last bunt in the second and Lover's steal, and Turkey's courage in not blowing up in those early innings, and Johnny's blazing speed and control when the chips were down, and—"

"Okay," Sleepy interrupted, remaining hurt, "I didn't amount to much—"

"But you did, Sleepy—you amounted to a very important part of a *team* that played a game completely over its head!"

Sleepy gave up. There were times when he couldn't get anywhere with his father—in moments like this and when his dad pulled that "balance of power" stuff. But later, alone on the porch, Sleepy found the copy of the *Press* and re-read twice more Dixie Bell's reference to himself. All-county! Sometimes on a sunny day when Sleepy closed his eyes two tiny spots of gold danced before his mind. That was how the words "all-county" lingered in his memory.

20 The
Hard Grind

READING DIXIE BELL'S stories in the Culver City *Press* now had become a daily habit with Sleepy. In the three weeks since Northfield's victory over Culver City, Dixie had begun a new Wednesday afternoon feature: "Candidates for the Little League All-County Team." McGillicuddy of Culver City and Abe Abelman of Franklinville were, of course, permanent fixtures on Dixie's weekly list, but so too was the name of Sleepy Jones. Each Wednesday Dixie added another candidate for each team, or dropped one in favor of another, and his nominees from Northfield presently read:

> Sleepy Jones
> Lover Carmichael
> Turkey Saunders

Lover sniffed. "I'll believe that guy's blathering when I see Poke Johnson's name there. And maybe Johnny's."

"Well, sure—Poke."

Lover looked around in surprise. "Good gosh, Sleepy, don't tell me you're serious about this idiot's stuff!"

"Well, no—not really," Sleepy said.

But he was.

"If you are," Lover remarked offhandedly, "you've at last found a common interest with Turkey."

"What's the matter with you?" Sleepy grumbled, and he broke into a scowl to hide his embarrassment. "Can't a guy even mention what he reads?"

"That kind of stuff—it would be better if a guy just forgot it," Lover retorted. "There are tree trunks in which anyone can carve his initials if he wants to be sure of leaving a mark on the future. Or he can wait till he finds somebody laying a new sidewalk and jam his foot in the wet cement."

Sleepy felt foolish, for when Lover spoke this way Dixie's weekly feature about candidates for the all-county team became a trifle ridiculous.

"As I see it," Lover added, "we win or lose as a team, not as a bunch of individual glory seekers!"

"Well, sure!" Sleepy admitted. He wished that his face did not feel so warm. Both his dad and Lover responded in the same tone toward what Dixie was doing.

"If anything could ruin the Little League," Mr. Jones had declared the evening before, "it is this sort of wrong emphasis!"

Buzz, on the other hand, took a more practical view of the matter. "Dixie only knows one approach to life," he said. "He's treating you as a bunch of pros—and to him the Little League has become strictly a form of public entertainment —which is a mighty tough racket, as nobody can know better than I. Dixie's technique is all very nice while your star is ascending, but the moment you begin to slip—watch out! You see, the craft of hero-making also includes the privilege of hero-breaking!"

"Without apology," said Lover.

"Oh, with something more than mere lack of courtesy," Buzz continued. "A hero who eventually fails you is simply a bum. You don't spare the whip. Whatever goes wrong, if you're a Dixie Bell you'll accept no part of the responsibility. So you prove your utter innocence by chopping off the culprit's head. It's quite a cosy business!"

Sleepy did not need to be a soothsayer to understand that Buzz, when he spoke, was remembering his own last days in professional baseball. Wasn't it Abe Abelman who had said Dixie had known Buzz during that sad experience? Obviously the man who once had led the pack braying for Buzz's blood now ruled the sports pages of the Culver City *Press*. Kelly would know; and Kelly instantly confirmed Sleepy's surmise.

"Aye, 'tis true. Dixie then was one o' the biggest shots in sports writin'. But, ye see, Dixie himself has slipped. Bein' sports editor o' the *Press* is not as big a job as Dixie held then. 'Tis the conceit o' the fellow that makes him overlook that fact. A verra interestin' circumstance, I'd say!"

Sleepy told himself that he better forget Dixie's self-appointed role every Wednesday as a hero-maker. At least on Thursday Dixie returned to being a straight reporter, giving the standings in the Little League and commenting on what he called "trials, trends, and tribulations." Three weeks following Northfield's triumph over Culver City, Dixie listed the Little League standings in this order:

Team	Won	Lost	Percent
Northfield	4	2	.666
Culver City	3	3	.500
Newton	3	3	.500
Franklinville	2	4	.333

Under "trials, trends, and tribulations," Dixie wrote:

> . . . The surprise has been this Newton team, which, losing three in a row and seeming completely outclassed, now has come back to win three straight. The wild game last week, when Newton defeated Northfield 9 to 8, is an example of the up-to-the-hilt style of playing in which Newton now indulges . . .

Sleepy would have preferred to forget that game. It had been more like a tussle between two pick-up teams than an organized League contest. Newton simply had made up its mind to keep plugging until it won; both Turkey and Johnny had pitched, and had been equally effective or ineffective, depending on how you looked at it. Everybody had hit on both teams, but Newton had scored one more run, and any other description of the game dealt with superfluous issues! Dixie's analysis of the Little League situation continued:

> . . . Northfield, splitting a two-game series each with Newton and Culver City and winning twice over Franklinville, leads the League, but now it must stave off this rather inexplicable charge of the Newton team. Life—and baseball—is not as predictable as we would like to think. At the beginning of the season, Culver City and Franklinville looked like the class of the competition, and Northfield and Newton appeared to be the woefully outclassed underdogs. Now just the reverse is true with the final round of competition about to start. Northfield and Newton will wind up the season in their final game, and—don't ask me why—thereby may hang the tale of the Little League championship! . . .

Mr. Jones, reading the same story, put aside the paper with a snort. "Dixie needn't worry," he said. "I'm not going to ask *him* why about the doings in the Little League or anywhere else! It's no mystery why Northfield and Newton are the race. They're the best teams!" And Mr. Jones grew as serious as though he was at the store explaining the virtues of a power lawn mower (something he couldn't afford to own himself) to a prospective customer:

"And what makes a team click? One star like McGilli-cuddy or Abe Abelman? No, sir! It's everybody's selflessness. It's Poke forgetting his head injury and getting back there behind the plate at the first chance! It's Johnny coming through in the Culver City game, but not pushing his weight around afterward! Johnny waits till he's needed; he's no 'twinkle, twinkle little star' that has to shine all the time! And it's Lover, and Hutch Bannister who goes on playing a good game at short without anybody slapping him on the back, and you when you forget this 'all-county' stuff, and—"

Sleepy said, reddening, "I get the idea."

Sleepy's father regarded him quizzically. "Do you really?"

"Yes I do!"

Mr. Jones winced a little at the sharpness that had crept into Sleepy's voice. Then, almost to himself, the man said: "Going on twelve—a tough age," and returned to reading his newspaper.

Another week went by; Northfield won over Franklin-ville and Newton defeated Culver City for its fourth straight victory; the hard grind of winning or losing the lead of the League on a single break gave no promise of changing. Sleepy lived in a world far apart from that of Mr. Trouble—or so he believed.

However, the existence of a three-year-old is, in itself, something of a hard grind. Surely its pattern is well fixed. Anything that already has happened occurred "yesterday"; anything still to happen will occur "tomorrow." Thus the past and the future are remote poles of the Universe, like the Arctic or the Antarctic; and the only reality is what is transpiring at the moment, for that is "now" or "today." In such a world, an hour is like a day; many moods can fill it, and also a considerable amount of curiosity. No one was more aware of this fact than Mr. Trouble.

The longest of the many days within a day that Mr. Trouble knew was the hour immediately following breakfast, when, bespattered with remnants of milk, orange juice, egg, and cereal, Mr. Trouble emerged from the kitchen with what Mrs. Jones described as "a Daniel Boone glitter in his eyes." All of the pioneer exploring ancestors whose ghosts haunted Mr. Trouble's family tree now crawled out on the branches, making their urges very much felt in Mr. Trouble's conscience. This was the hour when Mr. Trouble was most likely to pull out all the books on the shelves to see what was behind them, to sample the contents of any glasses carelessly left behind from the previous evening, to open all closet doors and bureau drawers, to empty any sort of box within reach (which is to say, *any* box not kept under lock and key or nailed to the ceiling), and to rummage through any ash trays, wastebaskets, and garbage cans that promised such delights as discarded razor blades, bits of candy, and wads of chewing gum.

Sleepy had been warned against this streak of the explorer that lurked in Mr. Trouble, and the door to his room, in fact, had been supplied with a hook-and-catch so that he might keep his personal possessions secure from the ever-eager invader. But a few days after the Franklinville game Sleepy's mind remained so absorbed with baseball that he neglected to fasten the hook-and-catch, and Mr. Trouble, finding that the door to Sleepy's room opened when he pushed, looked in upon the forbidden quarters and muttered: "Aaa-ba-ba-ba-ba!" This three-year-old code-language, in translation, said: "Brother, you'll sure pay for this oversight!"

And Mr. Trouble went to work. Thus, in a very short time, he brought into view the comic magazines Sleepy had stuffed behind the bookcase, found the penknife Sleepy had lost in a crack in the floor boarding six months before, disassembled a compass, upset a box of stamps and coins, unplugged the radio and three floor lamps, and demonstrated that without much effort at all he could push his finger through the tissue-paper wings of a model airplane. In the bottom drawer of Sleepy's dresser Mr. Trouble had just come upon a scrap-book when from below the insistent voice of Mrs. Jones reached him.

"Mr. Trouble, what are you doing?"

"Nothing!"

Mrs. Jones bolted up the stairs as though a demon with a pitchfork pursued her. Bitter experience had taught her that whenever Mr. Trouble announced he was doing "nothing" the roof could blow off the house at any moment.

"Nothing," hissed Mrs. Jones as she flew up the stairs. "You were doing nothing the day you disconnected the oil burner, and flooded the bathroom, and lost the cap from the gas tank on the car, and—"

The scene that met Mrs. Jones's gaze when she entered Sleepy's room couldn't have been any worse than she had anticipated; it was simply *that* bad!

"I'm good boy," announced Mr. Trouble, who proved his complete innocence by backing his hind quarters into the corner of the room between the bookcase and the radiator. "I'm good boy!"

Mrs. Jones sat down on the edge of Sleepy's bed and wanted to cry at all the unnecessary work the younger child had made her. She snatched the scrapbook from Mr. Trouble's hands. As the pages flipped open a certain guilty fascination seized her. It wasn't quite right to pry this way into Sleepy's private life, but, she rationalized, a mother had a duty to know what her son was thinking. And what Sleepy was thinking suddenly troubled her more than Mr. Trouble.

Mr. Jones now had formed a habit of returning a half hour earlier from the store at noon so that he could rest before lunch and combat the sluggish feeling that had bothered him earlier in the summer.

"He's saved every one of them," Mrs. Jones burst out the moment she saw Mr. Jones. "Every one of those silly stories Dixie Bell has written about him. He's got them pasted in a book."

"No!"

"Why does it have to mean so much to him? If he didn't make all-county now it would ruin his summer!"

"Yes, it might! Darn, Mother, I don't like this. It's the wrong set of values. It pits Sleepy against the team in a sense—makes him need to shine."

"I know—and I'm worried."

"What did you do with the book?"

"Left it where it looks as though Mr. Trouble dropped it."

"Good. Don't say anything to him either."

"I won't, but I wish—"

Sleepy, returning shortly afterward, accepted the spoilage of his personal possessions as the natural penalty for forgetting to fasten the hook-and-catch. The scrapbook promptly disappeared from public view.

Meanwhile Mr. Trouble put aside the entire incident as belonging to "yesterday." At the moment Mr. Trouble was fascinated at sucking his tongue. A lollipop tasted better, but sucking a tongue didn't take away its color or make it grow smaller.

21 *Crisis*

DESPITE the fact that a scorching August sun burned spots of brown in the best kept Northfield lawns, the signs were unmistakable that summer had entered its closing cycle. Merchants now advertised "end of the season" bargain sales on beach balls, bathing suits, cotton slacks, and fishing paraphernalia, and when Mr. Jones discussed his problems at the store he spoke of ordering rakes, storm sash, insulating wool, and other items for the fall trade. The grammar school on Maple Avenue received a new coat of paint in anticipation of another opening, a traffic light was being installed on Main Street so that when Padgett's awninged stand was dismantled this summer it could stay down forever (perhaps as a safeguard against the antics of any future Joannas), and at night when Sleepy lay in bed waiting for slumber to embrace him the croaking of the bullfrogs grew noticeably louder.

But more decisive than any of these indications that summer rushed toward a climax was the fact that only two more Little League games remained on Northfield's schedule—one against Culver City and the other against the blazing Newton nine.

"Two weeks," sighed Tennessee. "And two titles at stake."

For a moment Dodo Newson's sober face relaxed in an expression that, technically, could be described as a grin. "How many more four-leaf clovers do you need to save the world from disaster?"

"Only twelve," Tennessee replied. "One a day, if you count Sunday as a day of rest."

Hutch Bannister chuckled. "Can't you just see old Tennessee during the next two weeks? His nose will be rooting in the grass all the time!"

"Like a human ant-eater," agreed Lover, who laughed. And Lover orated:

> There is a tide in the affairs of men,
> Which, taken at the flood, leads on to
>   Tennessee
> With his snout rubbing in the dirt
> As he rejoins his noble ancestors!

"My great-great-great-grandfather," retorted Tennessee with dignity, "came from one of Northfield's finest families of earthworms. More distantly, we were related to the moles and the beavers, and, I believe, the scorpions."

"No good snail blood?" insisted Hutch.

"Only on my Cousin Lobster's side," Tennessee said. "She married an electric eel. Great seagoing folk, that side of the family!"

Sleepy chuckled with the others; to ruffle Tennessee required a deft talent—like the talent Culver City's McGillicuddy could display when pitching in a clutch. Sleepy sighed. Newton already had gotten over the hurdle of Culver City and had only Franklinville to glide past to reach its final game with Northfield, very much of a contender for the championship. If Northfield defeated Culver City the worst that could happen in a loss to Newton would be a tie and a play-off, but if Northfield dropped the Culver City game it could also drop the title to Newton in that one swift blow-up!

All the light-heartedness in the world over Tennessee's bid for the four-leaf clover supremacy couldn't disguise the seriousness of Northfield's situation. Even Buzz acknowledged it.

"This is the stretch drive," he said at practice, "the real killer-diller of organized baseball! The fans love its excitement, but for the players it's like sitting on the lid of a hot stove."

"Then tonight I get my mother to make me a pair of asbestos underdrawers," chirped Lover, who refused to be dismayed. At that moment the mystery of growth caused Lover's voice to sound both high and low. "Hey, Buzz," Lover said, "no wonder I'm good—I'm two people!"

Sleepy wished that he could feel as much at ease as Lover. Practice went badly for him. He seemed all thumbs the harder he tried, and he booted a grounder that he was sure he had judged properly. The poorness of his performance worried him, even though Buzz offered no criticism. And when on the Wednesday before the Culver City game Sleepy closeted himself in his room while he pasted into the scrapbook Dixie Bell's fifth straight reference to him as all-county material, the fretfulness remained. Gosh, if he tightened up now he could ruin everything!

Mr. Jones, deciding that evening that he'd like to challenge Sleepy to a game of checkers, couldn't find the boy on the porch.

"You rest here and I'll find him," Mrs. Jones said, and she set off followed by Mr. Trouble, whose day had now reached the cycle where he hugged a bedraggled Teddy bear as the only friend remaining in a world of gigantic, self-centered elders.

Sleepy had retreated behind the garage, where he banged a baseball against the board siding and dug hard after the rebound. Childhood superstition haunted him. Once he had counted telephone poles on the way to school as an omen of whether the day would be good or bad, a kind of variation on a moon-faced swain pulling the petals from a daisy and mumbling "She loves me, she loves me not!" At other times he used to forecast the nature of his luck by passing license plates—an even number at the end of the figure standing for good luck and an odd number for bad. Now if he handled five straight rebounds without a muff, he seemed to feel, he could go to bed without any more worry over the threat of that tightness.

The ball bounced awkwardly, but Sleepy reached for it with his glove and held on breathlessly. "Number four," he announced. One more to go! Damp hair hung across his eyes, and he brushed it aside with a hint of nervousness. Again he banged the ball against the garage, purposely giving himself no unfair advantage. A white streak flashed to his right. Sleepy flung out his arm in a desperate effort. But the ball, touching his fingertips, skittered away.

Sleepy felt so bad that he almost cried.

Mrs. Jones, watching the performance in silence, thought

that Mr. Trouble hugging his Teddy bear was not too much different from Sleepy. Her mother's heart was not very happy at seeing both her sons battling the sense of personal insecurity that must come now and then in all human experience.

"Don't you think you better come in?" Mrs. Jones asked gently.

"It isn't dark yet," Sleepy said, with a touch of open rebellion. "I—gotta—do—something!"

Mrs. Jones hesitated. Sleepy was ruining the back of the garage with the ball; she could make a reasonable issue out of that fact. Instead, she said rather lamely: "All right—but come in soon."

Back on the porch Mrs. Jones said to Sleepy's father: "Darn that scrapbook!" and felt like crying herself!

Sleepy's slumber proved restless that night; he never had caught those five straight rebounds! In the morning he acted cross at breakfast, and crosser still when Lover appeared suggesting another swim at the Y.

Lover, however, could grow bull-headed. "I told Tennessee and Shad we'd join 'em there. Poke and Johnny are coming too, and maybe Turkey. So you can just count yourself in on the party!"

Sleepy just couldn't think as quickly as he'd like so that he could shake Lover for the morning. And yet, hang it, he needed to sneak off behind the garage for another secret practice session—he had to catch those five straight rebounds the way . . . well, thought Sleepy honestly, the way Dixie Bell would expect!

"Now come along," prodded Lover, who was like a bulldog growlingly intent on ripping the seat out of a pair of trousers.

Defeated and sullen, Sleepy permitted himself to be led away, but afterward, in the stark naked privacy of the Y pool he was forced to admit, even though grudgingly, that he was glad Lover had driven him there. Tennessee's imitations of a seal and Johnny's inglorious belly-whoppers off the diving board brought a quick note of gaiety into the frolic. Turkey, an excellent swimmer, made the length of the pool under water. Soon they were all trying to equal Turkey's feat.

Sleepy, his lungs about to burst, conceded his defeat. Gasping and shaking the water from his eyes, he popped to the surface and clutched the side of the pool. A panting Lover already hung there, struggling to regain his normal breath, and next, like a pair of sheepish leviathans, Tennessee and Johnny labored over to the guide ropes similarly humbled.

At the sight of Turkey's exultant countenance, Johnny said derisively: "The more human you are the more nature draws you toward the sunlight."

Turkey giggled. "Look at Tennessee! The only thing he ever inherited from his Cousin Lobster was that green look!"

Sleepy began to laugh, and then the sound died on his lips and he grew painfully conscious of the awkwardness of his bedraggled nakedness. The door to the pool pushed open, and unexpectedly on the threshold stood Dixie Bell.

"The stretch drive, you know," the dapper little sports editor announced breezily. "Everybody's interested. Want to do a pre-game feature story on the Northfield team, so give with the copy, boys—old Dixie hasn't all day!"

If Sleepy were embarrassed in being so caught in the

presence of "Old Dixie," Lover was not. "What do you want to know?" the shortstop asked, thrashing water with his legs and driving Dixie back from the ledge of the pool.

"How do you fellows feel toward Buzz?"

"Like Trade toward Mark on a package of Smith Brothers cough drops," said Lover.

"I mean—"

But again Lover's thrashing legs interrupted the editor.

"'S a fact," chirped Lover. "We're all thinking of wearing false beards to prove it!"

A brittle edge of impatience crept into Dixie's voice: "Look, it's a long trip down here from Culver City. I'm giving you kids a break, so stop kicking those fool legs. I want serious answers!"

Sleepy couldn't blame Dixie for sounding stern. Lover was acting fresh. Sleepy said, "What do you want to know, Dixie?"

"How do you feel about this game coming up?"

"It's going to be tough."

"Who will Buzz start on the mound—Turkey or his own son?"

Lover cut in: "Buzz doesn't treat Johnny *as his own son* on the field!"

"No?" inquired Dixie, almost purringly as his brows arched.

"No," said Lover emphatically, "and for your information, Mr. Bell, none of us ever would think that Johnny's being Buzz's son would make the slightest difference whether or not he played!"

Lover's rising anger made his face grow ruddy, and to cool off the shortstop returned to swimming under water.

But Dixie's own cheeks had acquired a warmish look, and

Sleepy, anxious to avoid an open rift, said lamely, "I—I guess you better ask Buzz about the starting line-up."

Dixie wasn't easily mollified. "I guess I better ask Buzz *all* my questions, if I want to be treated decently," he snapped.

And the editor departed as unexpectedly as he had arrived.

At the end of the pool Lover popped out of the water, demonstrating that he wasn't too bad himself at imitating a seal. The sight of Dixie's disappearing coat tail pleased him immensely. "What d'you know," he said. " 'Old Dixie' got the idea. Nuts to that guy!"

Sleepy didn't meet Lover's gaze. They would pay for giving Dixie this brush-off, he'd wager, and for many reasons this reflection disturbed him. If he had stayed at home practicing behind the garage, as he had wanted to—

True enough, Dixie struck back in the pages of the *Press* next night—two cutting, dangerous sentences:

> . . . Success, going to the heads of the Northfield boys, will please both the Culver City and Newton teams very much. It would be too bad if Buzz's career as a Little League coach followed the pattern of his career as a major league player: a big flash and then an explosion! . . .

A sickness filled Sleepy as he let the paper slip onto the floor. He hoped that Lover was satisfied. He had ribbed Dixie and forgotten that the pen could be mightier than the sword! And Lover needn't worry any more about his appearance on the list of all-county nominees, for Dixie would take care of that. In his own case—Sleepy still hoped.

Lover's only contriteness was for Buzz. "You can see the kind Dixie is, needling Buzz that way!"

Sleepy, despite himself, nodded. There was a mean streak in Dixie all right.

Buzz simply laughed at the incident. "Dixie's slipping," he said. "He used to get a lot more fire into his abuse!"

" 'Tis only that he's out o' practice," Kelly averred. "Likely he's just warmin' up!"

Buzz shrugged and Lover looked relieved. Sleepy still wished the flare-up with the sports editor had been avoided.

On the morning of the Culver City game Tennessee Martin uncovered his forty-second four-leaf clover, and stood, he declared, on the threshold of immortality. In a sense, Tennessee said, he belonged with Eli Whitney and Christopher Columbus and Albert Einstein—men whose discoveries had changed the course of civilization.

"Not to mention Ignaze Iggleston," suggested Dodo soberly.

Tennessee confessed Dodo had stumped him.

"Ignaze," said Dodo, "discovered that by crossing eggplant with milk weed he could grow custard pies!"

"A fine piece of work," conceded Tennessee, without cracking a smile.

Even Dodo—or, for that matter, Ignaze Iggleston—couldn't deprive Tennessee of the notion that this was going to be his day. Nor, as subsequently developed, could Culver City's McGillicuddy, who watched Tennessee on successive trips to the plate pound him for a triple and a home run. Lover danced around exultantly, pointing out that not once had Dixie deigned to list Tennessee as an all-county prospect and yet the scoreboard showed four fat runs that Tennessee had driven in for Northfield! More important, said Lover, those runs would take the heart out of the opposition and from the dispirited droop to the Culver City boys as the third inning ended there seemed to be much evidence to support Lover's contention.

Sleepy certainly didn't expect any huzzas for his own performance thus far. Try as he would, he couldn't relax! Two errors in three innings—and silly errors, like dropping the ball after the tag on a pick-off play, and dragging his foot off the base on a perfect relay from Lover! If Dixie hadn't been huffed by the incident at the Y pool, this kind of playing still wouldn't have kept him on the all-county list! Sleepy avoided looking toward the crowd where last he had seen his dad and mother. It would be better if he never had kept that scrapbook! Well, he thought with a last tug of sadness, he could sure forget it now.

He was glad to have the inning over, and trudged into the Northfield bench with head hanging. Some dub, he was. He wished that he didn't have to encounter Buzz's glance.

The coach came across the field to meet him.

"Sleepy," Buzz said, "I guess we'll have to finish this game without you."

The first baseman's face flamed. "Buzz, I'll do better. Honest, I'll loosen up—so please don't yank me."

Buzz smiled softly. "I wish it were only that, Sleepy. It's your dad. They've taken him to the hospital. Your mother needs you, Sleepy, more than the team!"

For a moment the ground whirled dizzily around Sleepy. Why hadn't he known about this crisis? But the answer to that question was scarcely comforting: he hadn't known because he had been ashamed to look for fear his dad would understand why he had played so badly! And now—

Buzz's arm around his shoulder felt reassuring.

"Chin up, youngster. You know how to stand up to an emergency. You've already proved that to me!"

Sleepy swallowed gratefully. Then he broke into a run toward the hospital.

22 *What's a Team For?*

THE NURSE SAID: "It's a good thing we didn't wait any longer to remove that appendix. Mr. Jones was in real danger, and his condition, I suspect, had been building up all summer."

"He's all right now?" Sleepy asked anxiously.

The nurse nodded. "In another week he'll begin to feel so much like he once did that he'll seem five years younger!"

Mrs. Jones came into the waiting room. "Your father is doing fine," she said. "And now we better rescue Mr. Trouble from the neighbor who's caring for him and see that the poor boy's fed and tucked in bed."

For the first time since reaching the hospital, Sleepy realized how much the sunlight had faded. The game with Culver City must have ended hours ago; Northfield had led 4 to 0 when Sleepy had left, but with three innings still to play anything could have happened. Sleepy shook his head. This morning the outcome of that game had seemed the most important event in the world, but now all that really mattered was his dad's recovery from the emergency appendectomy.

Riding home in a taxi, Mrs. Jones said: "I must remember that your father wants me to call the newspaper and have them insert an advertisement saying the store will be closed during his illness."

Sleepy fell to sucking his tongue. Like Mr. Trouble, he found the habit conducive to deep thought.

Waiting on the porch of the Jones residence was Buzz.

"Everything go all right, Sleepy?"

"Dad's doing fine. How'd the game go?"

"Oh, we did pretty well. Tennessee found another four-leafer waiting his turn at bat in the fifth. So he did it again!"

"You mean he hit another homer?"

Buzz nodded. "And that sort of set everybody hitting. We finally won 12 to 0, which should give Newton some cause for reflection."

At the mention of the final game of the season Sleepy looked down at the floor. The issue had to be faced sooner or later, and the present moment appeared to be as good as any.

"Buzz," the boy said, "dad think's he's going to close the store, but he can't really afford to do that. I—I'm going to run it for him till he's well!"

"Good for you, Sleepy."

"Buzz, you can see how it is. So you better not count on me for practice—or for the Newton game."

The coach placed his hand on the boy's shoulder.

"Yes, Sleepy," he said, "I can see how it is."

Sleepy watched Buzz disappear through the first shadows of dusk settling along Maple Avenue. If the team had scored eight runs after he had left the game, it certainly could get along without his personal services! And only this morning he had thought of himself as the all-county first baseman, the indispensable man. That was a laugh all right! A little grim at the realization of what a conceited boob he had been, the boy went into the house to tell his mother of his decision in respect to the store.

"It would mean a lot to all of us if you could keep the business going," Mrs. Jones admitted.

"I'm sure I can."

"Still, Sleepy, giving up baseball with the championship game next seems like asking you to do too much."

"First things should be put first," Sleepy said firmly.

Mrs. Jones looked down at her son, who impressed her as having grown so tall this summer. A mist filled her eyes. Perhaps she remembered the boy behind the garage so nervously intent on catching five rebounds in a row—the boy who had seemed so much smaller. Mrs. Jones hid the huskiness in her throat with a burst of giddy, joyous extravagance. "I've got a steak in the refrigerator. Let's broil it for just the three of us!"

"Smothered with onions," Sleepy said happily.

On Monday morning, carrying Mr. Jones's key chain that must have weighed five pounds, Sleepy set off to open the store. When the lock turned, the boy told himself, "Enter Sleepy Jones, Northfield's new merchant prince!"

He looked around, deciding on his program for the day. First turn off the night light. Then remove the dust covers from the counters. The floor would need to be swept. But the thrill Sleepy anticipated was the tinkling of the bell over the door announcing the arrival of a customer. It would be something making that first sale—cash in the till to help his dad!

Sleepy had worked his way to the back of the store and was removing the last dust cover when the bell over the door finally rang. Sleepy rushed forward, filled with eager deter-

mination to make a sale. And from the threshold Lover
Carmichael greeted him:

"Okay, where's the broom? If I'm going to sweep the floor
I don't want any more dirt to pile up!"

"You—sweep—the—floor?"

"Uh-huh," said Lover. "The best little charwoman in
Northfield, that's me!" And since Sleepy still didn't understand, Lover explained about the meeting Buzz had called
the previous evening. "We're all going to help you—and,
brother, do we have ideas! Now this afternoon you and I are
on duty while the others practice, but tomorrow another pair
will take over while we practice. That way everybody will
miss only one practice session, which will be a good break
anyway, and on Saturday Kelly and Padgett will take over
while we meet Newton in tiptop form!"

Sleepy rested his back against a counter, not quite trust-
ing himself to speak. At last he managed to say: "The team
is doing this for *me?*"

"What's a team for?" Lover asked breezily.

Lover's broom had raised a cloud of dust when next the
doorbell tinkled. Kelly and Johnny entered. They walked to
the store window facing Main Street and contemplated the
collection of lawn mowers, sprayers, croquet sets, and other
merchandise on display there.

" 'Tis got to go," Kelly announced. "All this stuff!"

"And we'll need to put up a wire backdrop," Johnny said.

Kelly had started to remove a lawn mower from the
window when Sleepy shouted, "Hey, stop that—what do you
think you're doing?"

"A dense fellow," Kelly said to Johnny. "Can't he see I'm
clearin' this truck away?"

Johnny laughed. "We talked it over last night, Sleepy—how to attract attention to the store so that this week we'd be able to give your dad the best sales volume of the year."

"So I says," broke in Kelly, "what's the one thing in Northfield everybody'll stop to look at? The answer, me lad, is Joanna."

"And this window is where Joanna's going to spend her week," Johnny said. "I suspect it will please the little show-off, too!"

Lover leaned on his broom and chuckled. "I'm no fool! That's why I volunteered to clean up today. Tomorrow with Joanna around—well, it's Turkey's turn then . . . he can see what it's like!"

All Sleepy could say was, "Gosh!" He couldn't deny that Joanna would be a big attention-catcher.

Then Dodo and Tennessee arrived, lugging the sign between them.

"We worked on it half the night," Dodo said soberly, "so you better like it. It's for the window, and the fancy lettering is my dad's."

The sign read:

> Tomorrow
> This Store
> Will
> Specialize
> in
> MONKEY SHINES!

"That oughta get 'em," said Kelly.

"It sure should," Sleepy agreed.

"Of course," Lover added, in the matter-of-fact manner of a mercantile Machiavelli, "we haven't mentioned the

Rumor Brigade. That's Hutch, Shad, Poke, and Tennessee. Their job is to circulate through the crowds on Main Street and tell people, 'You better keep your eyes peeled on the Jones Hardware Store. Honest, it's going to be the best show in town!' As you can see," Lover went on, enjoying the grin that spread over Sleepy's face, "we aren't missing a trick!"

" 'Tis all for one an' one for all—except when yer fingers are in the cash register!" Kelly chuckled.

Within an hour the labors of the Rumor Brigade began to bear results. Many shoppers dropped into the store to ask "What's it all about, Sleepy?" and "When's the big unveiling?"

"Tomorrow."

The nice part was that they usually remembered a purchase they should make and the drawer of the cash register popped in and out with pleasing regularity. Lover proved the prize salesman, for his squeaky voice overruled all interruptions:

"Madam, a home with only one paring knife is a very sad abode. So you're late with dinner and you have both potatoes and onions to peel. Should you stop after the onions simply to wash a knife while everyone starves? Indeed not! Simply toss the used knife aside to wash later, and with this second knife breeze into those potatoes and—"

"You're silly . . . but give me the two knives!"

Not all the business of the Jones Hardware Store was done over the counter or under the pressure of Lover's piping exhortations. Toward mid-morning the telephone rang and a worried voice asked Sleepy, "Do you have a hand welder in stock?"

Sleepy checked and reported that he had.

"Good," said a relieved engineer. "This is the Northfield

Gas and Electric Company. Rush that welder right out here —every minute counts in fixing up an equipment break so that we don't have to interrupt service!"

Sleepy dashed off to arrange for the delivery. Once he had thought the things in his dad's store were so much miscellaneous junk, but now he could understand how hand welders and even paring knives were very definitely of importance to people. In a way, all of Northfield depended on the Jones Hardware Store for a part of its comfort, and if the store had been closed without warning for a week many persons would have resented that inconvenience—and rightly so, Sleepy told himself.

"'Tis ready," Kelly said late that afternoon as he drove the last nail to secure the wire backdrop. "Tomorrow we'll pack 'em in!"

Tuesday morning Sleepy awoke at dawn, dressed, and was frying his own eggs when Mrs. Jones appeared. "Here, that's my job," she said sternly, the way she might have spoken to Mr. Jones as the equal partner in a big enterprise— the running of a family.

Sleepy surrendered the skillet with a smile.

"Your father was tremendously pleased with yesterday's sales," Mrs. Jones said. "In fact, he thinks after his appendectomy heals he better have his tonsils out—just to keep you boys on the job a little longer!"

"Wait till tonight, after we spring Joanna on 'em!" Sleepy prophesied exultantly.

"It's a wonderful idea—except that Mr. Trouble wants to get in the window with her."

"Shall we let him?"

"No thank you. Joanna's fine—for you boys to manage.

Padgett ate it with pleasure.

That's in the right key and we'll leave it at that. Your father's reputation, on the other hand, is a grown man's reputation —for reliability, like delivering that hand welder when it was needed. Nothing you boys did yesterday meant more to him."

Sleepy ate his breakfast with the husky appetite that only a mind at peace can produce.

Turkey already waited to sweep the floor when Sleepy arrived with the keys, and Lover, eager to resume his selling, was not far behind, announcing that the Rumor Brigade had been ordered to perform an extra day's labor. Then Johnny and Kelly appeared with Joanna in tow.

Kelly hummed merrily:

> Joanna will shine today,
> Joanna will shine . . .

Down came the sign Dodo and Tennessee had fashioned. Into the window went the Rhesus monkey.

"The Jones Hardware Store," sang out Lover, "is open for business!"

Crowds formed early in front of the store. Joanna, always delighted at any audience, arose to the occasion. She strutted, she turned somersaults, she hung by her feet from the wire backdrop, she scratched her chest and stuck out her tongue at her sassy best. Laughter rolled along Main Street and drew more shoppers to gaze and to giggle.

But Kelly's sense of showmanship was not satisfied. His disappearance from the store was not noticed until he returned with Padgett. That the two Irishmen had hit upon a scheme in keeping with their native cunning soon became apparent, for Padgett's voice announced with gruff authority:

"I'll not have you blocking the sidewalk this way. Stop a moment, then off you go—or into the store!"

If there seemed an element of chicanery in this device for heading the crowds inside, Padgett speedily compensated for it. Since the appearance of a certain news photograph, the instinctive animosity between Joanna and the policeman had been well established. Now on the two sides of the window the foemen met once more.

Joanna played her role perfectly. As in the photograph, she placed her fingers behind her ears, then covered her eyes in the derisive gesture of blindness, and once, finding a flea, held it out in her paw as a peace offering.

But Padgett as an actor demonstrated no small ability. He shook his club, he placed his own hands behind his ears and wriggled his fingers, and he could, he now showed, display a broad piece of tongue if he was so minded. At the offer of the flea, Padgett responded disdainfully. Then, to Joanna's furious jealousy, he proceeded to peel a banana, and to eat it with an extravagant show of leisurely pleasure!

Inside the store the crowd giggled, roared, and offered boisterous suggestions for new frills to the performance. Lover had not listened to radio commercials for nothing. Now, mounting a chair, he made his steam-whistle voice heard even above this riotous din:

"Folks, the Jones Hardware Store always caters to your enjoyment . . . the show is free and the merchandise is moderately priced . . . every day, all the day, if at work or if at play, you can't beat the swell Jones way . . ."

Never, Sleepy knew, would business be better.

23 *Title Tilt*

AFTER LUNCH the crowds still gathered, and Sleepy almost regretted the practice that would take him away from the store from three o'clock until five. And yet who more than Buzz deserved his support—Buzz who had called the meeting that had sparked the team to help out at the store?

But, as Sleepy soon discovered, the influence of the store carried over into practice. Lover set the pattern, bellowing when he threw the ball to Sleepy:

"Here she comes—a box of bolts for Mr. O'Leary!"

And Poke, crouched behind the plate, fell into the spirit of the mimicry, singing out to Turkey, "Give 'em that old power mower pitch—the one that goes put-put-put as it breezes under the batter's nose!"

Buzz watched happily. So the championship game was coming up—what of it? His boys were relaxed, and that achievement was the first requirement of a champion!

On Wednesday, in the pages of the Culver City *Press*, Dixie Bell revealed that elephants were not the only mammals that held onto a grudge. After Tennessee had hit two home runs and a triple he could not very well be ignored as a nominee for all-county honors, but gone from this list, as though a blight had fallen upon the column of type, were the names of Lover, Turkey, and Sleepy!

"The old hero-maker," giggled Lover, "has only himself to blame—he's the one who picked us."

Tennessee bowed low, then stayed leaning over looking for four-leaf clovers.

"He's proving there are two ends to a hero," laughed Turkey at the sight of Tennessee's broad buttocks.

"My best profile," muttered Tennessee, without altering his position.

But Wednesday's column proved only a prelude to Dixie's symphony of bitterness. On Thursday the dapper little sports editor finally declared himself:

> . . . You must discount Northfield's one-sided victory over Culver City. The City boys simply folded—they were through, played out—and anybody could have beaten them. Northfield's overcockiness won't benefit from this experience. The logical pattern now—for the Northfield team, and for certain individuals we could mention of various sizes and ages—is to fade as even the beautiful rose fades as the end of summer approaches. So we will make two bold predictions. First, Newton will defeat Northfield on Saturday, even though the game may be close. Second, Newton will win the subsequent play-off and the championship. Sue me if I'm wrong . . .

"What can you buy in the Jones Hardware Store that symbolizes Dixie?" Turkey asked.

"Nuts," Lover answered promptly.

Sleepy told Buzz the truth. "I kept a scrapbook, that's how serious I took Dixie. I thought Lover was wrong the way he acted in the pool that day. Now—well, we should have dumped him into the water. Hat and all."

Buzz said, "Think there's enough chlorine in the water for that?"

"Gee, that's right—maybe that guy's rash of hate is catching!"

"We'll give Newton a good game," Buzz declared confidently. "If they beat us out for the title they'll deserve it."

At the store Friday morning Kelly said, "I dunno. Newton's got the drive o' a winnin' team, but so have ye. I don't deny that it'll be a tough game, but now I think Dixie's given ye an advantage. Dixie was among the loudest to howl for Buzz's scalp in Buzz's playin' days an' now he's howlin' for the scalps o' the team Buzz has coached. Ye see, Dixie's countin' on lightnin' strikin' the same spot twice, but lightnin's fickle stuff." And Kelly sniggered. "Reminds me o' the story o' a fellow who went out in a storm to see how well his lightnin' rod worked. The rod did fine. The lightnin' ran straight down, hit the ground, bounced off, struck the fellow in the pants, an' killed him!"

"You think we can be a thunderbolt in Dixie's case?"

"Aye. An' for this reason: Buzz has given ye the soundest groundin' in baseball o' any team in the Little League, an' when the goin' gets roughest 'tis the fine points o' the game that tell."

Practice that afternoon—the last before Northfield's title game against Newton—found Buzz anxious to avoid any sign of strain. No bearing down, the coach warned Turkey and Johnny on the mound; no swinging for distance, he told the batters. After an hour he called the team around him.

"We're ready," he said, "and now I suggest that you all forget baseball until we reach Newton tomorrow. Go over to the Y for a swim or help Sleepy at the store or hunt clovers with Tennessee—do anything that takes your mind off the game. You know at school there's a point where cramming for a test doesn't do any good but just tends to confuse you and make you tense, and the same principle holds true in baseball."

Buzz, bending over, pulled up a handful of grass that he stood fingering with a hint of embarrassed self-consciousness.

"I'd like to tell you boys how I feel about tomorrow's game," Buzz continued presently. "Win or lose, you fellows are still champions with me. When I came to Northfield the make-'em-and-break-'em school like Dixie had left me pretty sour—as Sleepy found out on that day he came over to borrow the bulldozer. I thought coaching this team would be a bore—just something I had to do if I wanted to be accepted in a new town—but I soon got rid of that silly idea. I simply had met a lot of new friends in you boys—friends I enjoyed and respected and wanted to be with. Through the season that feeling has grown, and when the season is over I want you to know that for any of you at the Kyler household the latchstring always will be out. Come whenever you wish, and it will be a privilege for me to have you."

When Buzz concluded, the old field was silent. Sleepy swallowed hard and blinked his eyes against tears that welled up in a surge of great emotional warmth toward Buzz. Little Lover also blinked, and Dodo hooked a finger over his nose as though he was trying to find a place to hang his face where it couldn't be seen. Sleepy reckoned that it must be a little past four. Twenty-four hours hence at least half of the Newton game would have become history. What, Sleepy wondered, would be their attitude then?

At exactly five minutes past four on Saturday afternoon, Sleepy discovered, Newton was still at bat in the last half of the fourth inning. The scoreboard read 0 to 0, but that situation promised soon to change. There was only one out, and a Newton player, who had walked when Turkey's control weakened momentarily, now rested on second following a sacrifice fly. At the plate stood Newton's shortstop, a strapping, blond-haired lad named Jacobson, whose muscular arms said "power hitter." Sweat ran in sticky streaks along the surface of Turkey's high cheekbones.

Sleepy, pounding his glove, calling out encouragingly "Easy does it, old Turkey-trot!," wished he could feel more at ease himself. The crowd that jammed the Newton ball park was even spread out along the fences in the outfield. A special table had been constructed behind the backstop for Dixie Bell, and here the sports editor of the *Press* sat with hands poised like a hawk's claws above the keys of his portable typewriter, ready to swoop down and record the tale of disaster that might impend.

Sleepy pounded his glove once more and recognized the faces of Abe Abelman and McGillicuddy in the spectators behind first. This game was the pay-off all right; partisans from every team in the Little League had been drawn to the title tilt. And now the crowd fell silent, as though in a moment of expectancy all breathing had been suspended.

Lover called out, "That's Jacobson up there, Turkey. He's got one glass eye and can't see out of the other!" But Lover's voice cracked.

Turkey rocked back on the mound, and on the Northfield bench Buzz twisted a blade of grass around his finger. The ball streaked in and Jacobson swung. Sleepy's heart sank.

The ball would drop in for at least a double—the run would score—and, in truth, the Newton boy who had been on second already had crossed the plate when Lover cut off Tennessee's throw at short.

The Newton supporters sounded hysterical. Turkey looked sick. Sleepy walked over to join Lover at the mound.

"It's as good a pitch as I can throw," wailed Turkey.

"It's only one run," Sleepy said.

Turkey squeezed the rosin bag and looked down at the plate. The batter now was the Newton catcher—a boy who was chunky like Poke, and as level-eyed and as stubborn in his purpose. That purpose was clearly to pound in another run or at least get on base. Turkey gulped; he could feel the batter's intensity out here on the mound. Sleepy returned to first and Lover to short. Jacobson bounced down off second, hooting and anxious to rattle Turkey.

Still Turkey didn't throw. Then he appealed to the umpire for time out, and Sleepy saw the pitcher walking over to the Northfield bench to talk to Buzz. When Turkey started back to the mound it became obvious what he had said: "I haven't got it, coach. Johnny better warm up."

Johnny rose and slipped on his glove.

Sleepy thought: "Turkey voluntarily confessing he's finished—Turkey *asking* for relief while there's still a chance!" Sleepy's heart went out to Turkey. He was playing honest with the team!

The Newton catcher also doubled and Jacobson scored. Poke came out to the mound to join Sleepy this time. Hoots and catcalls, shrieks of jubilation and shouts of booming confidence ripped the linings on the throats of the Newton fans. The big 2 that dropped down on the scoreboard after the name of the home team looked as imposing as Pike's

Peak on a sunny day. Dixie Bell's fingers flew across the keyboard of his typewriter.

"Walk this next guy," Poke said.

"The pitcher?"

"First is open, anyhow. Fill it and we'll have a play at any base. Who knows?" Poke said. "A double play has pulled us out of a jam before!"

But Sleepy wasn't fooled—nor Turkey. What Poke really meant was that an intentional base on balls was the safest course Turkey could pursue to provide a few more precious moments while Johnny unlimbered his arm. In a way, Sleepy thought, Poke was heaping humiliation on Turkey. The jeers would rock across the field when the batter was purposely passed. Turkey drew a deep breath. His face seemed flushed.

"All right," he said.

The sarcasm of the Newton adherents was even worse than Sleepy had expected.

"The monkey's up a tree!"

"Quiet, fellows—this is Be-Kind-to-Dumb-Animals Week!"

A glum silence settled over the Northfield rooters.

With a face almost crimson, Turkey stuck to his task, pitching deliberately and slowly and allowing Johnny two or three fast warm-up pitches for every ball thrown to the plate. At last the chore was completed. The Newton batsman threw aside his stick and trotted down to first. Turkey stuffed his glove into his hip pocket and began the long, painful walk to the bench. The hoots grew louder. Johnny stopped him, and held out his hand.

"You're quite a guy," Johnny said.

But Turkey couldn't answer. A wetness filled his eyes.

Poke demanded another conference at the mound. Sleepy heard Johnny ask, "How do you want 'em pitched?"

"Low," Poke answered shortly.

Johnny's head jerked around. "Nothing doing," he snapped. "One hospital case a season is all I'm good for."

Poke's chin jutted out. "Who calls the pitches on this team?"

Johnny said, "But—but—"

"But-but yourself," Poke answered tersely. "You sound like a run-down motorboat!"

Before Johnny could protest further, Poke turned and ambled back to the plate. But the catcher's conference at the mound, Sleepy noticed, had achieved at least one encouraging result.

Poke had left Johnny in a sweat.

24 *No Heroes Wanted!*

EVEN ÐIXIE BELL had stopped pounding his typewriter, and his face, like Buzz's on the Northfield bench, looked tensed and strained. But what Dixie couldn't understand, and Buzz could, was the signal Poke gave as he dropped two fingers below his mitt and chest protector.

Johnny took a hitch in his belt, still hesitating. Dixie Bell grinned, reading the wrong meaning into the moment. So, too, did the Newton rooters, and their hoots now simply were transferred from Turkey to Johnny.

"He'll blow up, too!"

"This is kite-flying day in Northfield!"

Poke repeated the signal; he wanted that slow slider that began to fade away halfway to the plate. Johnny surrendered. His head fell in a brief nod.

Dixie Bell, Sleepy thought, choked up with the emotion of the moment, never tried to report the *real* story. Lover hopped around, on edge. Hutch Bannister's throat gurgled.

But Poke stayed crouched low, cool and determined. Just

once he pounded his mitt, then held it raised. Johnny kicked up his leg.

Poke went down on his knees, and the swinging bat of the Newton player at the plate seemed to graze his head. Grinning, Poke cocked back his arm with the ball clutched in his hand.

"What d'you know?" he called out to Johnny. "*I caught it!*"

Johnny shook his head. It seemed like suicide to him, but if this was what Poke wanted—

A change had come. Sleepy could sense it first within himself, in the way his stomach settled back to its normal depth. Maybe in the pages of the Culver City *Press* the Northfield team wasn't very heroic, but this, by golly, was a team where everybody played the game for all it was worth, and no heroes were wanted.

Even though Newton led 2 to 0, a change had come. Sleepy could sense it in the tightness of the Newton batter, in the way visiting players in the crowd like Abe Abelman and McGillicuddy leaned forward with eyes popped open, in Poke down on his knees again—under that swinging bat, holding onto the ball. As Dixie might have written—and had written about the Northfield team, in fact—the Newton rally was about to fade "as even the beautiful rose fades as the end of summer approaches."

A change had come, for on the Northfield bench, for the first time that summer, Buzz stood up. Those were his boys out there—Poke and Johnny and the others—and everyone was like a son! Buzz cupped his hands to his mouth, and, perhaps taking a hint from the Newton fans, demonstrated that he could rip a little lining off his own throat.

"You, Poke! You, Johnny! That's baseball, by golly! *That's all-Northfield baseball!*"

Poke scrambled after a pitch, flat on his belly. But the ball was in his mitt. The ball, Sleepy knew—they all knew—would be in Poke's mitt every time! The Newton team knew it, too —one more sign that a change had come!

Turkey leaped up from the bench when the inning ended. There was yet a mistiness in Turkey's eyes, but there likewise a change had come, for it was a different sort of mistiness. Turkey raced out to the plate and threw his arms first around Poke and then around Johnny. But Lover was more unashamed. He picked up the ball and kissed it.

Buzz said, "That makes up for everything—for every rotten incident in the minor leagues . . ."

But the final note of the total change that had been won belonged to Tennessee. He was the last to reach the bench, for an important discovery had delayed him.

"Mr. Buzz," Tennessee said, holding out the clover, "I give you Number Fifty—the world's record, all classes included— the most immortal single symbol of good luck known to man, civilized or otherwise!"

"Tennessee, what do I do with it?"

"Eat it and for the rest of eternity you will have a charmed existence."

Dutifully, Buzz ate it.

A walk and a single had put Tennessee and Lover on base when Sleepy came up in the top of the fifth. A feeling spread through Sleepy's bones. Once before against Newton—

On the way to the plate Sleepy passed the table where Dixie sat. For an instant the boy paused and his eyes met those of the sports editor. Deliberately, Sleepy winked.

Buzz noticed. And as an ex-Yankee, Buzz remembered one of baseball's most immortal legends. Goaded one day by the boos of the fans, Babe Ruth had stopped swinging his bat and pointed to the part of the fence over which he intended to hit the next pitch for a home run. And that was what the great Babe did.

Sleepy passed on to the batter's box. Dixie, puzzled, gazed after him. Sleepy dusted his hands. He felt loose. He felt good.

And then he felt better. His bat caught the pitch. He knew that ball was gone—over the fence—a souvenir for some cow to nibble on! He circled the bases with his heart singing. Northfield 3, Newton 2—but there would be more. And maybe now Buzz would tell him what Buzz had shouted at Poke and Johnny. Anybody in the Little League had a chance to make Dixie's all-county team, but to only a few was given the privilege of playing on Buzz's all-Northfield nine!

Sleepy's foot touched home plate, the figure 3 flashed up on the scoreboard for Northfield, and the cheer that rolled from behind the bench of the visiting team grew like the waves of the ocean on an incoming tide, beating harder, growing more thunderous with each new surge.

Buzz waited a little distance in back of the batter's circle. When Sleepy reached the coach, the man's arm went around the boy's shoulder. Sleepy remembered twice before when Buzz's arm had meant so much—the day of that bus ride and on the afternoon his dad had been rushed to the hospital.

"You know," Buzz said, laughing, "I never digested a four-leaf clover so fast before in all my life!"

Before Sleepy could answer, a new wave of cheers swept through the Northfield rooters. A parade was forming down the side of the field—led by Joanna on her chain and by Mr. Trouble atop the shoulders of Turkey's father. Then the banner was unfurled, and at the sight of the fancy lettering Sleepy suspected that here once again was evidence of the handiwork of Tennessee's dad. The banner read:

ALL AROUND THE BASEBALL PARK
THE MONKEY CHASED THE WEASEL!

The picture of Joanna on the banner was labeled "Northfield," while across the image of a forlorn and lachrymose weasel was scrawled "Newton."

Buzz grinned. "When the weasel thought 'twas all in fun," he said, "the *pop* he heard was your bat smacking that homer, Sleepy!"

Sleepy could not but admire the artistry that had fashioned the picture of the weasel, for the animal's long, pointed face bore a distinct resemblance to the angular countenance of a certain well-known sports editor!

25 *"The Shiningest Monkey"*

THE FINAL MARGIN of Northfield's triumph over Newton was 5 to 2, and the Victory Banquet that the merchants provided for the team was held a week later in the gymnasium of the Y. Parents and even the younger fry like Mr. Trouble attended, and in the spirit of equal justice to all Joanna's cage was set in the middle of the speaker's table with an honor guard of Kelly on her right and Padgett on her left.

The Rhesus monkey munched happily on bananas supplied by her two guardians, while the others feasted on fried chicken, on mashed turnips and candied sweet potatoes and fresh limas and sliced tomatoes, on corn on the cob and gallons of milk, on home-baked rolls and blueberry muffins, on ice cream and cake and—for those, like Dodo and Shad, who had no bottoms to their stomachs—sliced watermelon.

Sleepy demurred at the watermelon. "I used to think I had an appetite," he said, "but now I don't know."

So contented and so convivial had grown the inner man of Lover Carmichael that an overwhelming sense of gratitude prodded him to his feet. "Ladies and gentlemen," squeaked Lover, "I feel constrained to say a few words . . ."

Poke and Hutch seized Lover's coattail and pulled him back into his chair. Everyone laughed.

Then Mr. Jones stood up, seeming to glow with health now that he had recovered from the main shock of his appendectomy.

"Ladies and gentlemen," Sleepy's father said, without anyone seizing his coattail, "the merchants of Northfield decided among themselves some weeks ago to give to the player who best exemplified the spirit, the ideals, and the aspirations of the team—the player, that is, whom Buzz selected upon this basis—some type of special award. And this is what we decided upon."

Mr. Jones held up a perfect miniature in sterling silver of Joanna.

"Now," Sleepy's father went on, "without revealing just yet the name of the recipient, I should like to read you the inscription: *'to the shiningest monkey of 'em all. . . .'*"

Again the laughter was general.

"Character, of course, was the key requirement," Mr. Jones said. "And growth—"

Sleepy thought: Poke will get it. Poke deserves it. The way Poke had shaken off that bad injury, and then forced Johnny to throw him those low pitches . . . well, you just couldn't say Johnny didn't deserve it, either. He had won some fight within himself—

"—we thought, too," Mr. Jones was saying, "that we couldn't give the award on the basis of any one game. It was the season as a whole that counted—"

Sleepy thought: on those grounds you couldn't ignore Lover, old Mr. Emergency himself, the squeak that had become a spark. Or Tennessee, who had really pounded that old apple when it counted most. And, good gosh, Turkey—the way he had taken himself out of the Newton game—

"—on purely technical grounds," Mr. Jones continued, "we barred Kelly (laughter) from the award, although in a quiet way his service was unselfish and enormous (loud cheers). So, too, did we bar Padgett (cheers again). Of course if we were to pick a person who brought these boys together determined to do or die we might have to consider Dixie Bell (cries of 'Hear! Hear!' and boos). Now give the devil his due (laughter). Unselfishness was a prime factor in making a choice—"

Sleepy thought: Hutch, too, quietly, unspectacularly, had measured up. And Dodo and Shad. But Lover, Johnny, or Poke—it had to be one of those three. Or maybe Turkey—

"—and so," Mr. Jones said, "with some pride that you will understand, I come to the choice—"

Sleepy understood then. His face started reddening.

"—this boy fought many battles: within himself, all alone. Buzz says he grew up twice in one summer—"

Sleepy hated to look at Lover or Poke or Turkey or Johnny. They deserved it more. But they were all looking at him. And grinning.

"—moreover, this boy learned to give something up for another and—"

Lover could stand the suspense no longer. His steam-whistle lungs exploded:

"*Yeah, Sleepy!*"

Then Poke and Johnny and Turkey and Hutch and Lover and Dodo and Tennessee and Shad were pounding Sleepy's back and shaking his hand and mussing his hair.

"You old Sleepy-britches, you!"

"You old son-of-a-gun!"

"What's the matter with Sleepy?"

"He's all right!"

Tennessee and Dodo started the chant: "Speech! Speech!"
Sleepy stood up. His legs wobbled. He opened his mouth.
No words emerged.

Lover leaped to his feet.

"Ladies and gentlemen," cried Lover, "if Sleepy has nothing to say maybe I could speak a few words—"

This time when Poke and Hutch seized Lover's coattail they dragged him down on the floor and sat on him.

WORLD *Junior* LIBRARY

Exciting, action-filled, inspiring and always engrossing, WORLD JUNIOR LIBRARY books will delight all boys and girls who love good reading. These are quality books by famous authors, in handsome, clothbound library editions.

TITLES NOW AVAILABLE

JILL'S VICTORY *by Elisa Bialk*

THE SUN-DOG TRAIL *by Jack London*

SMOKE BELLEW *by Jack London*

JEAN CRAIG GRADUATE NURSE
by Kay Lyttleton

PAT'S HARMONY *by Page Cooper*

GHOST GABLES *by Mildred A. Wirt*

THE PAINTED SHIELD *by Mildred A. Wirt*

WILD STALLION *by Bud Murphy*

BULLARD OF THE SPACE PATROL
by Malcolm Jameson

FAVORITE DOG STORIES
edited by Marguerite Bloch

COMANCHE *by David Appel*

MONKEY SHINES *by Earl S. Miers*

THE WORLD PUBLISHING COMPANY

CLEVELAND AND NEW YORK